Brecht's Mistress

Brecht's Mistress

Jacques-Pierre Amette

translated by Andrew Brown

THE NEW PRESS

NEW YORK
LONDON

Requests for permission to reproduce selections from this book should be
mailed to: Permissions Department, The New Press, 38 Greene Street, New
York, NY 10013

Originally published as *La Maîtresse de Brecht* by Editions Albin Michel,
Paris, 2003
English translation first published as *Brecht's Lover* in the United Kingdom by
Hesperus Press Limited, London, 2005
Published in the United States by The New Press, New York, 2005
Distributed by W. W. Norton & Company, Inc., New York

LIBRARY OF CONGRESS CATALOGING-IN-PUBLICATION DATA

Amette, Jacques-Pierre, 1943-.
  [Maîtresse de Brecht. English]
  Brecht's mistress / Jacques-Pierre Amette ; translated by Andrew Brown.
  p. cm.
  ISBN 1-59558-019-0
  1. Brecht, Bertolt, 1898-1956--Fiction. I. Brown, Andrew, Dr. II. Title.

PQ2661.M4M3413 2005
843'.914--dc22   2005050505

The New Press was established in 1990 as a not-for-profit alternative to the
large, commercial publishing houses currently dominating the book
publishing industry. The New Press operates in the public interest rather than
for private gain, and is committed to publishing, in innovative ways, works of
educational, cultural, and community value that are often deemed
insufficiently profitable.

www.thenewpress.com
Designed and typeset by Fraser Muggeridge

Printed in the United States of America

10 9 8 7 6 5 4 3 2 1

To my sister

Underneath them are gutters,
Inside them is nothing. And above them, there is smoke.
We lived in them. We enjoyed them.
We soon died away. And slowly, they too are dying away.

Bertolt Brecht, 'Cities'

East Berlin
1948

For a long time he gazed out at the forests and their russet colours slipping past.

At the frontier between the zones, Brecht climbed out of the car, went into the German police post, and telephoned the Deutsches Theater. His wife, Helene Weigel, took a walk round the car to stretch her legs. An armoured truck was rusting in a ditch.

An hour later, three black cars came to fetch the couple. There were Abusch, Becher, Jhering, Dudow – all members of the Cultural League. They explained that the press were waiting at the railway station and Brecht said, 'That way we're rid of them!'

He smiled. Helene smiled, Becher smiled, Jhering smiled rather less and Dudow didn't smile at all. Her arms loaded with a bouquet of daisies, Helene Weigel stood erect between the officials. She had a black suit, a bony face, a severe gaze, and hair drawn back in a bun: she was smiling and inflexible.

Bertolt Brecht shook hands with a few people. White faces. Grey faces. The couple remained motionless amongst the long coats of the officials of the Cultural League.

Everyone seemed rather awed by Brecht, this round-faced man with his hair combed forward like a Roman emperor's.

To see the great Bertolt at last, the most famous German playwright returning to German soil after fifteen years of exile!

When the last photographer had been pushed away by one of the policemen, Brecht slammed the car door shut and the convoy of official cars swept off.

Brecht gazed thoughtfully at the tar on this road that led to Berlin.

You do not enter the city, you enter a grey and shapeless mass.

Obscene graffiti, trees, grass, great neglected rivers, overhanging balconies, unfamiliar plants, and stunted apartment blocks rising in the middle of fields.

The car entered the heart of Berlin. Women in headscarves were numbering stones.

He had left German soil on 28th February 1933. At that time there were banners and swastikas in all the streets... Today was 22nd October 1948. Fifteen harsh years had passed. Today, the official cars sped along, overtaking Soviet lorries and the few, shabbily-dressed pedestrians.

Brecht lowered the car window and asked the driver to stop. He got out, lit a cigar and gazed at the ruins. There was a vast silence, patches of white wall, blackened windows, countless buildings in a state of collapse. The evening sunlight, the wind; many curious butterflies; dismantled artillery batteries; a blockhouse.

Brecht sat on a stone and then listened as the driver told him that if only the financiers would get in on the act, they'd be able to rebuild the city more quickly; and Brecht reflected that it was precisely the financiers who'd caused the city to be flattened in the first place. He got back into the car; the street walls cast long shadows across its interior.

Mile after mile of rubble, glass roofs in smithereens, armoured vehicles, roadblocks, Soviet soldiers standing in front of *chevaux de frise*, and barbed wire fences. Some apartment blocks resembled grottoes. There were craters, huge expanses of water and more ruins, vast, empty spaces, and occasionally a group of pedestrians, gathered around a tram stop.

The staff at the Hotel Adlon watched his arrival through the windows.

In the big hotel room, Brecht took off his gabardine and jacket. He showered, and chose a shirt from his suitcase. Four storeys down: German soil.

There was a welcoming speech in the hotel salon. As they thanked him for being here, Brecht drowsed and his mind wandered; he was thinking of a very ancient German folk-tale that he'd read at school in Augsburg and later remembered during his stay in California. A serving girl had noticed a familiar spirit sitting near her by the hearth; she'd made room for him and chatted to him during the long winter nights. One day, the serving girl asked Little Heinz (the name she had given the spirit) to show himself under his real identity. But Little Heinz refused. Finally, as she persisted, he agreed and told the serving girl to go down into the cellar, where he promised to show himself. The serving girl took a torch, went down into the vault and there, in an open barrel, she saw a dead child floating in its own blood. Many years before, the serving girl had secretly given birth to a child; she had slit its throat and hidden it in a barrel.

Helene Weigel tapped Brecht on the shoulder to bring him out of his torpor – or rather, his meditation. He sat up straight, put on a brave face and reflected that Berlin was a barrel of blood, that Germany, ever since his teens, at the height of the First World War, had also been a barrel of blood and that he was the spirit of Little Heinz.

There had been bloodshed in the streets of Munich, and modern Germany had been swamped in the rivers of blood that flowed through the old Germanic folk tales. He had come back into the cellar and what he now wanted was, with his modest reasonableness, to pull the child out, educate it, and wash away with cold water the blood that still lay on the cellar flagstones. Goethe had done the same with his *Faust*, Heine with his *On Germany*; but the stain was now bigger than ever; Mother Germany was half-drowned in it.

Through the windows he could see women in big coarse shoes numbering stones. There weren't any streets left, just broad roads and clouds.

Later, in a room at the club of the Cultural League, there was a brief, intelligent speech by Dymschitz.

Brecht looked with amusement at Becher, Jhering and Dudow. What an ill-matched, amusing trio, he thought through his cigar smoke. There before him were the men whose mission it was to guide East Germany towards the grandiose conceptions of the

Artistic Fraternity. Two of them had been companions of his youth. Now they had become 'comrades'.

Imagine three men in dark overcoats with white shirts and polka-dot ties. These men – in the main hall of the Seagull Club, dressed in outfits cut from some dreadful Soviet cotton. Dymschitz was reading from three sheets of grey paper. He was as refined as a university professor who, having been appointed rector, keeps an eye on his figure in the hope of seducing young women.

Next to him was Johannes Becher. He hadn't changed. Round glasses, with lenses for myopia: he was still as gentle and kind. Becher for his part remembered the young Brecht, slim, discontented, his hat on his head, a black cigar in his mouth. His feet propped up on a chair, reading or rather crumpling the pages of the Berlin newspapers, well pleased at the idea he had managed to rake in loads of money really quickly with *The Threepenny Opera*. Brecht was busy learning all about 'war economy' from a little blue hardback book; he wandered around carrying anatomical drawings, and wanted to buy an axe to smash in the heads of those wimpy numbskulls who managed the big Berlin theatres. He would run after trams, and climb onto the theatre rooftops, a cabaret girl hanging on each arm. He intended to present the audience with gigantic social struggles. The problem? He still hadn't had time to read Marx, but he believed in Marxism with every fibre of his being – it was such a huge fund of ideas for his plays. And, as Dymschitz read his speech of welcome, Becher was wondering, deep down, whether old Brecht had hidden an axe under his coat today. To smash the skulls of the official writers of the GDR...

Johannes Becher, now a high-ranking figure in the eastern zone's cultural politics, was thinking of the young Brecht's impeccable leather coat. He wondered whether Brecht's skin had by now become thick enough to confront the 'comrades' who were experts in Marxist opinion, the 'specialists' who ran the redoubtable Writers' Union.

Helene Weigel, too, remembered Becher. For her, what had changed about Johannes was his back: it was so straight now, and he kept his body in trim, like an army officer. In bygone days he had thrown cherry stones into the hair of actresses as he lounged full length in a hammock. Helene thought, 'I'll get on better with Becher than Brecht'.

Paler of face, with his rather round, smooth head, and the darting, isolated, lucid, refined expression in his eyes, Herbert Jhering delivered a short speech. He turned the pages and read out from his small round handwriting with courtesy and detachment. The speech was full of facile, pleasant-sounding formulae.

Brecht remembered that, once upon a time, he had read Jhering's drama reviews the same way you listen to the diagnosis of a doctor you esteem. Jhering was already the most esteemed and feared of critics.

As he'd grown older, he had assumed the demeanour of a diplomat. But his eyes had lost their twinkle.

He hadn't had to hang around for long before being denazified. There was a lack of people with intelligence of his level who could be used to rebuild a policy of education for all. As he continued to deliver his compliments to Brecht, in sparkling style, the atmosphere in the room remained chilly. He drew to an end, his voice husky, calm and gentle. Then he held out his left hand and placed it on Brecht's shoulder to remind him that he'd been his companion ever since the start of his career. With his hand he was touching the sacred substance of their youth. There was another speech.

Helene Weigel, who was listening pensively and rather wearily, leant her head towards Brecht and murmured in his ear, 'Who's that fat guy over there, the one holding his hat in his hand?'

She indicated the man who, massive and balding, drenched with sweat, was wearing a tight jacket that wasn't properly buttoned up. He sported the enormous cuff links of an ostentatious shopkeeper, and was standing to attention, as if he could see German Virtue flooding the room with its blinding light.

'Dudow! That old crook Dudow!' replied Brecht.

He too, Slatan Dudow, had worked in Berlin in the twenties, he too was a companion from the Golden Age, when everyone was out on a spree in the wonderful Berlin of easy women and pleasures you could buy just by dipping into the ever-flowing streams of money gushing from the cash registers of theatres on the verge of bankruptcy.

This Bulgarian had worked on the screenplay of the film *Kühle Wampe*, around 1926 or 1927. In 1932 he had guided Brecht through a Moscow already subject to police surveillance. Brecht reflected, 'He must provide them with just the kind of politically correct artistic work they expect... probably gone soft in the head... he must come first every time in the political arse-licking contests...'

He smiled at Dudow. Everyone applauded when Becher embraced Weigel and Brecht.

White wine was served.

Later on, at the Hotel Adlon, the telephone rang (it was a huge, ancient contraption that seemed to have come from Soviet army surplus), but it was Weigel who answered. Everyone wanted to see Brecht: Renn, Becker, Erpenbeck, Lukács.

A floor waiter brought a tray overflowing with congratulatory telegrams. From behind the smoke of his cigar, Brecht continued to gaze out placidly and ironically.

Night fell.

Brecht stayed sitting alone in his room. He stared at his new pass.

2

The Met Office of the Soviet Army had been set up
in an old private house in Luisenstrasse, not far
from the Seagull Club where all the official repre-
sentatives of culture would come along to chat,
read the papers and swap the latest news. Behind
the patch of wasteland there were four huts that
belonged to the Soviet military administration. They
were home simultaneously to a visa service, several
offices of Radio Moscow, and various additional
services that ceaselessly amassed huge volumes of
reports arriving by lorry from the former Luftwaffe
ministry.

Bringing the letter that had summoned her, Maria
Eich entered the second hut, the one whose windows
were covered by wire mesh, and pushed open a
wooden door with a glass pane in it. She found herself
in a corridor dimly lit by electric bulbs, with several
trolleys bearing piles of old *Signal* magazines and
well-thumbed files with labels for school exercise
books stuck on them. The labels bore purple-ink
inscriptions in Cyrillic characters.

Maria continued down the corridor. She was
wearing a grey waterproof. The pallor of her face.
Through a half-open door, a woman could be seen,
in an austere grey suit, with her hair in a bun. She was
sorting through a pile of paperwork.

'Excuse me, I was looking for Hans Trow's
office?...'

Without replying, the woman turned round to Maria and pointed to the end of the corridor.

The two windows were covered by thick wire meshing. Two Soviet soldiers moved aside to let her through. Old military maps and plans of Berlin from the ex-ministry of the Luftwaffe, doors with curious steel bolts, plywood panels set against the partitions covered in a carpenter's thickly-pencilled shading: it was all redolent of repair work, improvisation, poverty, with the inadequate light coming from naked bulbs hanging from twisted flexes held in place by nails.

When she went into the room that was just lit by the wire-mesh window, a girl was perched on a ladder and pulling out files from a washing basket. She then slid them into place on a shelf.

Hans Trow, in a thick roll-neck sweater, blond, sporty-looking, was rubbing his neck as he leafed through reports written in Russia. He was annotating certain pages with precise, rapid little gestures. A smell of glue and dried book-bindings. The girl, perched on her ladder, came down and scrutinised Maria's face as she went by.

Hans held out his hand.

'Maria Eich?'

'Yes.'

He pulled over a chair and placed it so that Maria would be sitting with her face to the light from the window, and he would be against it. Then, after sending his assistant away, he spoke in a half-indolent, half-ironic voice.

'My name is Hans Trow. I look after people travelling between zones.'

He lifted up a bundle of bulletins on economic data and pulled out from under it a dossier bound in grey, which he flicked through. Inside it were stapled pages of typescript and crumpled sheets of carbon paper.

Hans Trow got up, came round and propped himself against the front of the table. There he stayed, motionless and smiling.

Then he slowly looked up and, throwing himself back a little, scrutinised this young woman with her ravishing face. He noticed she had clean-washed hair and a very pale complexion, and, above all, that her hands kept changing position. Hans Trow took no pleasure in making this young woman feel uncomfortable. He found that, for an actress, her face had an astonishing clarity. So what was Maria Eich thinking of? Her modest, somewhat melancholy air surprised Hans, as it didn't tally with the file sent from Vienna, where they spoke of Maria as a brilliant, classy actress, 'full of energy, with a real taste for the social whirl'. Finally, Hans seized a beige cloth-covered file, took from the drawer a thick pencil in chestnut-brown wood, and leafed through the file as he spoke without affectation or animosity.

'It's a nice name, Maria Eich.'

He didn't raise his voice as he continued to turn the pages of the file, marking certain typewritten phrases with a cross from his brown pencil. On her side, Maria Eich replied to an initial series of questions on her childhood, her Viennese past, and the start of her career, all the time wondering why this intelligence officer was speaking in such a monotonous voice, his delivery neither speeding up nor slowing down. She found that his somewhat weary courtesy was worrying. She sensed a hint of mockery when he asked her why she was the 'protégée' of a man as important as Dymschitz.

'You are his protégée,' he repeated. 'His protégée... Comrade Dymschitz runs the whole cultural sector... You've known Dymschitz for five months... Where did you meet him?'

During the questioning, Maria had the impression that the officer who had introduced himself as Hans Trow (in the same way that men click their heels in Prussian barracks) held all the evidence to prove that her family had been in cahoots with Nazi circles in Vienna, since he had, right in front of him, the National Socialist Party membership cards of both her father, Friedrich Hieck, and her husband, Günter Eich. Hans Trow had turned the pages of the file as he recited the details of the precarious situation of her father, a refugee in Spain, and her husband – he resided in Portugal under an assumed identity that the East German intelligence services were perfectly well aware of.

Having dwelt at length on the destiny of a father and a husband both of whom he described as 'Nazi nutcases' who deserved to be locked away in a 'lunatic asylum', Hans, with his frank, clear, straightforward gaze, offered her what he called a 'general guarantee for the future'.

Weighing his words very carefully, instead of playing twenty questions (Hans already had all the answers in his papers), he proposed that Maria work on 'changing the history' of this country. He immediately started talking about citizenship, treatment, salary, medical care, supplies, decent accommodation and the furthering of her artistic career. Just as in a film where a gambler in the casino wagers his last remaining money on red, Maria heard herself accepting all these terms. Unless she did so, she would be forced to flee through the obstacle course of bridges, streets, and barriers, before she could reach the western sector, only to find herself in front of American officers who would throw in her face a whole pile of overwhelming evidence of the Nazi pasts of her father and husband. Her situation would be even more precarious in West Germany; she would be carted off from the barracks to some awful army theatre, unable to claim any support or any protection. She would have no security for her little girl. She would be under suspicion, spied on, kept under surveillance, she would be fair game for pimps. She imagined the endless attempts at bribery. All those humiliating scenes, yet again. She saw herself penniless, her name covered with shame – while here, Dymschitz, the man in charge of cultural affairs in the Soviet zone, was her 'friend'. There was a series of short sharp clicking noises from Hans Trow's lighter as he lit a cigarette and then toyed with it. She heard him as if through a fog assuring her, 'You were Dymschitz's mistress'.

She wound a coil of her hair round her forefinger.

'Do you really want to know? No, I never slept with Dymschitz…'

'Fine, fine, fine.'

He cleared his throat.

'One day…'

Just then, a man of about thirty came into the office. He was podgy, with his hair slicked down with brilliantine, his shirt collar rumpled, and an old-fashioned cardigan with missing buttons. He wiped the sweat off his forehead with a big check handker-chief. He mumbled a vague 'hello' to Maria, as if presenting his condolences. He looked for a chair and found one behind several files on the subject of coal allocations and the recycling of stocks of gloves and boots.

With his rumpled outfit and his black stringy tie round a threadbare collar of dubious white, the man, introduced by Hans Trow as Theo Pilla, his assistant, resembled the porter of a pre-war Berlin hotel. His greasy hair made him look like a dead body just pulled out of the water. In disillusioned tones, Theo Pilla, without paying any attention to the visitor, muttered, 'Those never-ending conversations on wheat and coal with the leaders of the CVJM, the Christlicher Verein Junger Männer, are starting to wear me out…'

He pulled a piece of crumpled blue paper out of his pocket and unfolded it with a slight cough. He said, 'Do you know this Dietrich Papecke?'

'No,' said Hans, cross at being interrupted.

'I just need to have a little chat with him, otherwise it'll be back to earthing up spuds in Schwerin for him.'

Hans tapped his finger in perplexity, and performed the introductions.

'Theo Pilla, Maria Eich...'

'You the actress?'

'Yes,' said Maria.

Theo gazed at this slight woman with a scarf draped sensibly over her coat, and her delightfully blond, curly hair. He felt embarrassed in the presence of this pretty woman who was doubtless disguising her worries behind an intense, anxious frostiness. While Hans spoke, Theo slipped a piece of cardboard under a window that was letting in the rain; then he wiped off the trickles of water with a corner of his jacket.

Hans resumed, 'So you don't have any special relationship with him. You know we know about it. The lonely position you find yourself in...'

'You're wrong, I don't feel lonely.'

'But...'

'No, I'm never lonely.'

'Sorry?'

'It's the plain truth,' continued Maria, 'I never feel lonely, never!'

There was a certain wavering. Hans Trow restrained his smile and wondered how to make contact with her, how to break her pretty little armour of pride.

'You know why you've been asked to come here?'

'No.'

'Our idea might be put in these terms: we need to rebuild this country with people we can rely on. We can't allow ourselves to return to the days of Weimar...'

The rain gradually slackened off and there was now only a faint dripping in a gutter. Theo Pilla mechanically arranged rubber stamps in rows and said, 'We're not out for revenge. Quite the opposite: we think that the new Germany needs to come to maturity, to endorse new principles, and we want actors to show a bit of political passion, to understand our interests and to support the positive elements as against that whole jumble of reactionary ideas still cluttering up people's minds. You understand?'

Hans continued, 'The state of mind – control of the state of mind... You understand? It's all in line with what you would like, and what Comrade Dymschitz would like... Yes?... The liberation of Germany... It's already come about on the military level... but today it's the political level that's at stake... it will happen thanks to you, and us...'

Theo came and sat next to Maria.

'We are rebuilding the real Germany. There won't be any unemployed, nobody will be humiliated, there won't be any provocations or denunciations, but we must be vigilant. You'll be a militant. You'll be one of us. We won't rebuild a militaristic Germany... In the other Germany, half the Nazi criminals are planning their revenge... They're already eating nice warm pretzels with the American generals; it's obvious they're ready to demand justice as they shake their butcher's aprons! In our system, we need a vanguard that can influence and educate our comrades, purify people's hearts, give them work, bread, dignity... You must help us!... the same way as you must listen to Brecht. You'll be his confidante. We'll finally find out who he really is!...'

'Don't you trust him?' said Maria, taken aback.

'To tell you the truth, we absolutely haven't got a single thing against him. We'd like to know – and we're going to find out – who he is. Is he a real "comrade"? He chose the United States...'

Theo paused, and pulled out a horrid-looking little cigar.

'You have a child in West Berlin...'

'For now, Lotte is living with her grandmother.'

'Where?'

'In the American sector, the other side of Charlottenburg.'

'Yes, I've got the address. Why is she in the West?'

'Lotte has asthma. The Americans have good medicines... for asthma.'

'That's fine then,' said Hans. 'You'll be able to see your daughter Lotte whenever you want.'

He opened the cupboard and pulled two documents out of a box of chalks. A pass in grey cardboard, crossed in pale red, and a receipt for signature.

When Maria signed the receipt with Hans' pen, Theo said, 'You're one of the family now'.

'You'll have accommodation and a personal dressing room in the Deutsches Theater,' added Hans.

'We need to know who Brecht is... What he's thinking about...'

Maria raised her pale eyes and became flustered.

'But... But...'

'You simply need to get close to Brecht. You'll see, in the evening, Brecht will come for you in your dressing room, you just have to open the door for him... Sometimes you'll have to listen to him, sometimes ask him a few questions. You know that, over there, the Americans – they're preparing for war, yet again. We want to know who he is. All that time he spent in California... He left Germany such a long time ago... Go and find out who he is. Find out. He's a great man, but he might have changed. His place is so important, but is his spiritual greatness up to the task we are entrusting him with? That's what we want to know. You'll help us.'

'Why me?'

'Everyone must have a mission in our new society, to make sure the horrors of Nazism never return. The war is still going on, Maria Eich...'

'There's no harm in living with a great man,' said Theo, relighting a cigarillo.

'Are you seeing anyone right now?' asked Hans.

'Nobody.'

'Good...'

Maria bowed her head in perplexity.

'If you want coffee, sugar, wood for heating, blankets, meat, silver knives and forks, a nice washbasin, just ask…'

Theo put his pencil down.

'There's no question of you being a useless person in our society. "Hearts that are pure and ardent",' repeated Hans Trow, 'that's what we need.'

'Everything can be arranged with a bit of goodwill,' added Theo Pilla.

Before she stepped through the office door to leave, Theo Pilla gave her an address in Schumannstrasse so that she could have her lungs X-rayed. There was so much tuberculosis around – the lack of milk and meat, the poverty.

The next day, near a canal, sheltering from the downpour under a huge lime tree, officer Hans Trow instructed Maria in the new geopolitical situation entailed by the partitioning of Germany and the catastrophic imminent rearmament of West Germany. He drew from his pocket an official document written in English, a confidential copy of the seminar that had been held in the monastery of Himmelrod, in the Eifel region, during which certain ex-Nazi officers had envisaged leading the Federal Republic of Germany into an offensive 'defence' against the Soviet zone…

'An offensive defence… you understand, Maria?'

Hans said, 'Everyone in Berlin is walking around in rags! Instead of tons of coal, a few paltry planks torn up from the parquet floors of the old Reich ministries, burning in the few braziers around. Everything to do with coal and petrol, and the transportation and arrival of essential foodstuffs, depends on the Russians. We depend on the Russians. It's Moscow that makes the decisions.'

'Will Moscow make a decision about our theatre?' asked Maria.

'Why are you asking that? It's the wonderful good fortune – more than we'd hoped for – of our great new brotherhood,' said Hans Trow laconically.

Sitting on the bench next to Maria, Hans was a scrupulous teacher, showing his pupil that the world is divided into good and bad, and that the battlefield is wherever she happens to be. Maria needs to convince herself that she is in the midst of the best troops; the country must not fall into the hands of a gang of criminals, and she must stick to her place in the fight.

'You mustn't be afraid,' he added. 'Artists bear a very heavy responsibility for having helped bring in the Nazis. They were scared of the SA bawling in the streets, they capitulated and stayed in their dressing rooms, applying their greasepaint. A generation of stooges. Maria, you won't be a stooge!...'

There was a silence, and Hans murmured, as if coming out with an improvised confession, 'We are still in thrall to bourgeois thought. That's going to change...'

Hans also explained to her that there were military actions aimed against East Berlin.

Between simple artistic militancy, and being a new recruit to State Security, there was but a step. She took it.

Sensing that his future recruit was a 'pure and ardent heart', Hans Trow draped her waterproof over her shoulders. He smiled. He dropped her off at the Seagull Club.

3

As she entered the dining room of the Seagull Club, Maria Eich gazed round curiously. Wearing a long black coat with an astrakhan collar, she made her way over to the master's table. Brecht, for his part, looked like a parvenu peasant who has hung his cap on the branch of an apple tree.

He had his eyes closed as he savoured his cigar. He listened to Caspar Neher, his faithful set designer, the oldest and most faithful of his friends – they'd known each other at school in Augsburg in 1911, and had never lost sight of each other since then. 'Cas,' Brecht called him. Right now, he was showing him several photographs of the production of *Antigone* at Coire, in Switzerland. Screens draped in red cloth, props and masks hooked on a rack, an impression of empty space and matt lighting. Brecht focused with particular attention on the horses' skulls in papier mâché.

'Lighting to be sharp and uniform.'

He seized on two snapshots in which the barbaric acting space was framed by half-light.

'No! Sharper! More uniform!'

'Half-light looks better behind the posts and the horses' skulls,' said Caspar Neher.

'No. A cold lighting will help the actors…'

Caspar Neher, his forefinger poised, indicated the ball of haziness that extended behind the posts.

'And here?'

'It's already too shadowy,' Brecht judged. 'The audience shouldn't have to ask any questions apart from those that the characters onstage are asking themselves. Cas, you need to take out that shadowy bit that hides the backcloth. No black hole. No daydreams. Cold, hard light. In all this half-light you could easily imagine crimes, intrigues, people hiding. You can cut someone's throat in it, or dream of a forest on the march. No!'

Brecht turned to Maria and called her to witness.

'The actors in Shakespeare's Globe only had the chilly light of a London afternoon!'

The light falling slantwise from a window illuminated Brecht's upper face. He spoke with a Bavarian accent, somewhat gravelly and slow.

His evocation of the theatre to come had awoken in him all the good things in the life he had led in Berlin in the twenties, when his fame was assured and the *Threepenny Opera* had been such a runaway success. 'Look at the street,' he continued, to no one in particular, as if he hadn't heard Neher. 'It's so close to us that lots of people don't notice it... the street... the street...'

He turned to Maria.

'If you want to know about theatre,' he said, 'you don't need poetry.'

He added, 'You just need to stay in touch with the streets. Poor streets, rich streets, empty streets, full streets!'

Later on, in his car, Brecht took a few notes. It seemed to him that all the women in Berlin had grown old. His hand trembles, the town passes by, sudden glimpses of the canal, smashed factory windows, sombre walls, rubbish. Cars, pedestrians, avenues, desolate railway stations, all reach out to the dead.

'Your onstage make-up should be lighter, more Chinese. Less expression in your face. I'll explain…'

They reached Schumannstrasse, near the rehearsal room. The black Stayr drew up outside the porch of a former clinic.

Someone pulled out a Leica – Caspar Neher. They went into an old arched courtyard, darkened by a glass gallery with broken panes. The little group, with Brecht at Maria's side, moved close together and stood motionless for the family photograph. The golden haze made the foliage stand out with statuesque solidity. A sense of warm space. A moment of hesitation in the group. A sudden emptiness. The speed of rotation of a half-dead planet, bringing back the golden shores of the past, the mischievousness of vanished generations.

'Allow me to introduce my next Antigone!' said Brecht. 'Maria Eich!'

Weigel came towards Maria with a face as blank as a whitewashed wall and said, 'A Viennese like me'. Young, healthy, she thought. A lamb flung to the wolf. A flirtatious appearance, the rebellious nose of young women who wearily receive the homage of men. She has nice supple hair, mine is grey. She's young, I'm old! Another affair that will soon be over and done with… it won't last long.

Helene said drily, 'Rehearsals on Monday!'

For three days, Brecht introduced Maria to everyone he met.

'This is Antigone! Her name is Maria Eich...'

A field full of rubble. Berlin resembled a deserted beach. One evening, in the Café Berndt, Brecht pulled a notebook out of his pocket and with his propelling pencil drew a circle with odd-looking posts. He picked up a glass and round its base pencilled in some horses' skulls.

'This is the area in which Antigone will perform.'

He shaded in the circle.

'You will perform here. The other actors will be sitting on benches. Here.'

Later, returning from the toilets, he sat down again, and scrawled another drawing, hairy and obscene. The kind of drawing you find on WC doors.

He burst out laughing.

The next day, they went up Charitéstrasse. Brecht trudged stolidly along, the pavement belonged to him. He was a peasant returning to his farm. He suddenly sat down on a bench. He closed his hand round Maria's hand. The sun cast Brecht's shadow onto the bricks of a grimy apartment block. Brecht was heavy of figure. He took off his glasses to wipe them with his handkerchief. Maria took his glasses and handkerchief. She wiped them and saw for the first time the fatigue, the reddish eyes, the shadows under them that maybe indicated a cardiac illness or quite simply the approach of old age. Brecht said, 'All Antigones, until now, belonged to the past, spoke about the past. You're going to be the first one to speak about us... without indulging in aestheticised, petty-bourgeois Hellenism. How are we to bury our German sons? How?'

Maria understood nothing of what he was saying.

4

While Maria familiarised herself with the rehearsal rooms of the Deutsches Theater, fitted out her apartment and joined in all the meals with the actors in Brecht's circle at the Seagull Club, Hans Trow, for his part, plunged night after night into the study of the files sent by the Moscow base. He would sometimes climb up to the top storey in the building, and take a corridor that narrowed and led under the eaves to a padlocked cell to which only Hans possessed the key. Inside, the wallpaper was covered with damp patches, the plaster was crumbling, there was an old radio set and heaps and heaps of files written in Russian that Hans would sort, open, read through or put back into a metal cupboard.

For whole nights, Hans Trow would sit on the stool and examine, sort out, leaf through, annotate and pin together these notes emanating from Moscow. There was lots of material on Brecht's habits, the people he saw, the peculiar interest he took in the struggle waged by atomic scientists against the state, the way he procured money for himself from a Swiss bank (the same one used by the film director Fritz Lang), the way Brecht would cut out pages from magazines, anything to do with agrarian reforms in the Soviet Union, his meticulous vigilance in noting the acts of corruption perpetrated by the European bourgeoisie of different countries who had collaborated with Hitler's Germany, his bizarre fascination for everything to do with nuclear research, his way of cutting any articles on quantum physics out of the science journals, his disquieting fierce hostility to the monopoly held by the military both in the Soviet Union and the United States, as well as – and this made Hans Trow smile – his lubricious notes on American actresses, and the account he kept of the sexual feats of his Swedish mistress, Ruth Berlau, now an alcoholic.

So it was all collected in an iron safe to which only Hans knew the combination. Thus, after several months of sleepless nights, Hans Trow knew everything about Brecht's various sojourns in exile. His first period in Denmark, then that lovely thatched cottage in Lindigö, Sweden, when Brecht, still euphoric, optimistic, boastful, would jot down in his notebooks reams of idiotic judgements about the 'Moscow clique', since the major Soviet theatres kept putting on plays by authors he disliked, in productions he described as 'dismal crap'. Then the house in the middle of the birch trees in Finland, anxious that he might not be granted a visa for the United States, the sleepless nights listening to the radio and the presenter spouting Hitlerite propaganda while Brecht moved the little flags showing the shifting war front across the wall map.

The only thing that made Brecht feel really afraid was when he crossed the Soviet Union to reach Vladivostok. He was haunted by the fear of being arrested in Moscow – a fear that was evident and omnipresent. Trow was stupefied. The Moscow base depicted him as a man of the theatre whose Marxism was primitive. This mountain of paperwork described an aesthete rather than a politician, an artist fascinated by gangster plays, detective stories, Luther's considerations on the Devil, irrigation systems in Ancient China. Sometimes, Hans Trow would detach a note and slip it into the leather briefcase which, in the morning, he took to his office on the second floor. He would pass it over to Theo Pilla who, in turn, typed out with two fingers the contents of these notes, on a long-carriage typewriter he'd found in the former Luftwaffe ministry. They drew up a report for Becher, who handed it on to Kubas, who sat on it for three days before sending the entire pile of bumf on to the office of the great, the mighty Dymschitz, the man in charge of cultural politics for the entire GDR.

Theo Pilla spat on 'that whole pack of actors hamming it up, poncing around, with their taste for revolutionary art' – they were there to 'bore the shit out of the working classes' with their performances of *Faust* or *Iphigenia in Tauris*: that was how he put it. How extraordinarily incongruous it all is, thought Hans Trow, in the morning, when he took his shower in the building near the stadium, in front of the canteen. Curiously, he never entrusted Theo Pilla with the big files from Moscow that contained the reports of those who had sheltered Brecht in Finland, nor the improbable notes of the FBI, accompanied by blurry photos.

Hans Trow also gathered and sorted the documents provided by a British air hostess. There were also some papers that did not concern Brecht directly, but had been assembled in Boston by the FBI. There were a lot of notes on exiles who were suspected of secretly belonging to the Communist Party, in particular František Weiskopf, who had been a member of the Czech CP.

For two weeks, Hans loosened his tie and painstakingly went through the notes of a certain Johnny R. who had spent his life on the cocktail circuit and hanging out at the wild parties of Hollywood film people, especially Charlie Chaplin and Fritz Lang. He passed himself off as a trainee assistant, which didn't fool anyone, and he shut himself away in the toilets to jot down in a notebook everything he heard about those exiles who'd all known each other during the Weimar Republic. There'd been Anna Seghers, the Communist writer, the producer Edwin Piscator, who'd always found it difficult to get on with Brecht at the time of the *Threepenny Opera*, and Ferdinand Bruckner, who'd translated *The Lady of the Camelias* and worked with Helene Weigel on a play by Hebbel in 1926.

What made Hans Trow smile, as he leafed through these notes, was imagining Fritz Lang, Brecht, and Helene Weigel all strolling down Sunset Boulevard. In the evening, they chattered away on the flat roofs as they watched the dusk fall. Flashy cars driving along in never-ending streams... Hans Trow would pick up a cigarette and take a deep puff, then plunge back into the notes. He could see Chaplin and Brecht walking along the Pacific. The white sails of yachts glided along the horizon. Then Chaplin and Brecht would meet up with Groucho Marx and they'd listen to the results of Roosevelt's re-election as the sun set over the ocean.

Here, night was falling, Berlin was fading into the blue shadows, shot through with tremulous lights. Hans picked up one last typewritten letter that was lying in the file labelled 'Exiles', and methodically unfolded it, taking long drags on his cigarette. He recopied in a notebook all the figures relating to the considerable loans taken out by Barbara, Brecht's daughter, from American bankers. He finished his evening by scattering the ashes from the ashtray into the coal-burning stove and meditating on the anti-Semitic jokes that, according to the FBI agent, circulated among artists. He switched off the three lights in the office, then the corridor, and said good-night to the sentry at the foot of the stairs.

Outside, it was raining, The snow was melting.

5

Once he had finished typing out the report on his long-carriage typewriter, podgy Theo Pilla pulled the page out from the roller. He reread it: 'Already feeling guilty for falling in love with a Nazi who was no good for anything more than picking up sticks, Maria Eich has taken refuge in work and is forever striving to become the one great actress of the Deutsches Theater, finding a sort of consolation in her unremitting efforts.'

He felt he had just composed a clever little memo that summarised his sources nicely; then he wolfed down a small pork pie with a daub of mustard. He also drank two glasses of beer, heaving several sighs of contentment. His face was ruddy-cheeked, and his eyes moist, as he observed dusk falling. From the window he could see the headlights of the lorries rumbling through the American sector. By way of relaxation, Theo flicked through *Neues Deutschland* and came across a photo of Brecht taken outside the Deutsches Theater in the company of several actors. He thought: he's a peasant, like the ones you find in Grimm's fairy tales. He'll swap a one-eyed goose with you in exchange for a cow, and make you think you're getting a bargain.

Theo opened his black briefcase and slipped into it the latest numbers of *Neues Deutschland*: they were singing the praises of Communist youth, the nation's spearhead.

He went out. A gust of wind heavy with rain, a poplar tossing and swaying in the wind. It turned into a spectre, in a whirlwind of leaves; in the evening, the ruins grow longer, and empty the earth of its meaning.

It was after a lunch at the Seagull Club that Brecht had taken Maria to visit the villa at Weissensee. This isolated residence in the forest, by the lakeside, was built in a neoclassical style, with a Greek pediment, columns, and a flight of steps covered by a glass canopy which, every winter, trapped the rotting leaves.

The black Stayr drove down a muddy avenue.

They went inside the house, after spending a long time trying to find the right key on the bunch.

The strong musty smell took them by surprise. They pushed back the inside shutters covered with spiders' webs, walked over parquet floors covered with dead flies, and climbed the big marble staircase leading to the first floor; they went through many dark rooms. They lowered their voices as they spoke, wandered through the spacious rooms still wearing their coats, and sat for a while in the living room downstairs, watching the branches through the old net curtains stretched across the window. It was then that Maria kissed him. He pulled away.

'Don't kiss me!'

They faced each other. No shared past. What happens right in front of our eyes is absolutely not what happens in our hearts. I'm going to sleep, walk, live, sleep together with this man, she thought. For Maria Eich, Germany was a new country, a series of green hills lined by birch forests, ruined motorways, clouds; for Brecht, it was a country to be rebuilt with money. A field for experimentation, a laboratory for an ideological revolution aimed at the younger generation. Neither of them had this country in common.

In the numerous empty rooms, everything was bathed in a grey haze made of dust and the afternoon gloom, as Brecht leant against a marble mantelpiece. The dim magnificence of this neoclassical dwelling, the deep but threadbare gold of the old wall hangings, was proof to him that Dymschitz and the others had decided to think big and treat him as the country's official artist.

Then he watched Maria Eich consuming segments of an orange; there was something disturbing about her; the orange slices disappeared into her mouth, and he thought: a solitary little squaw. She must huddle up quickly on a sofa the minute she's been undressed. He felt that he was a sumptuous fakir and told himself that it was pleasant to know that actresses of around twenty-five or thirty are very thick on the ground and that you can mix them all up together and fuck all of them.

He lit a cigar. His generosity would consist in using Maria Eich as part of a theatrical aesthetic that would make her more interesting than most other actresses. He wasn't much of a decent bloke in bed (he thought, 'time to hit the hay'), but he was always generous on the well-lit stage of a theatre, and he would turn this Viennese bauble into a formidable Antigone. She was charm personified, they would both eat at the same table, sleep in the same bed and never think the same thing at the same time. And this would be delightful, for a while. She was smiling, dainty, blond, pale-complexioned, charm personified...

He took a few steps towards the hall. She had taken off her coat and merely draped it over her shoulders. She took a walkabout too, and discovered an old junk room at the end of a corridor. There were old earthenware plates, with depictions of asparagus in relief. There were also some forks and little spoons in the drawers of a kitchen table and, curiously enough, chicken feathers, as if a child had once upon a time collected them.

Brecht was standing in silence in front of a window and gazing out at the ash trees. The world had changed; all that was left of Germany were cities exposed to all the winds, and men and women of good will.

Maria came back with a blue plate.

'Look, here's a nice one...'

Brecht vaguely replied, 'Very nice.'

'Who lived here before?'

'Before what?'

'Before us.'

'Before us?' he repeated.

He lit his cigar.

'Nazi crooks, I imagine.'

The remark astonished Maria. Bertolt Brecht was already rapping on the window pane to attract the attention of someone who was wandering round in the garden.

Suddenly, the afternoon clouded over, leaving Maria with little more than a sense of decomposition. She was useless, out of place, a dress stuck on a coat hanger. She listened to words, saw objects, walked around, but everything was in chaos, and if anyone had asked her to talk about what she was feeling, she would have described herself as a being cast astray in an insubstantial world.

Brecht noticed how pale she was. A flood of tenderness overwhelmed him when he saw her so fragile, so defenceless, over there by the window. He went over to her, as she was positioning her left shoe in a ray of light, as if to test its solidity.

'So what's wrong?'

He placed his lips on the collar of her blouse.

'You're not on trial, Maria!…'

Later, they drank tea, having located a kettle furred over with lime scale.

Brecht kept his cap pulled down tight on his head. Maria felt that she was being swept away by events that left her incapable of responding. He was thinking that he'd ended up with a rather complicated actress. They suddenly felt the cold. They went back to an isolated café not far from Friedrichstrasse, one of those gloomy places with a single big round table, covered with an immaculate white tablecloth. This whiteness carried a secret message.

The place was desolate and yet comforting with its roaring stove. Brecht pulled a pen out of his coat, a block of paper, and drew a circle: he was with his Antigone again. Maria watched his hand tracing the performance area. In a destroyed city, there was a hand drawing, detached from everything. Brecht's pen moved slowly and formed parallel lines that turned out to be upright posts; the pen hung suspended. Brecht said, 'Caspar Neher will be able to draw the horses' skulls – I can't.'

Then he drank his coffee, and didn't wait for Maria to finish hers before saying, 'We've got a meeting at the Deutsches Theater…'

It was abominably cold outside, but Maria was relieved not to be in the little room with its odour of stale cigar-smoke hanging in the air.

Columns of Soviet lorries were rolling by, then there were crossroads, a canal, shadows, carts, and a rubbish dump, vast in size. The evening slowly closed in, and a low rumble of thunder, just one, echoed over the city. Brecht slowed down and stopped the car outside the porch of a courtyard that had remained more or less intact. There were a few coats standing round a brazier. A woman was waving a piece of cardboard to drive off the acrid smoke and make the embers glow red.

'Look at those poor people,' said Brecht, 'look at them, just look at them!… Refugees in their own country, refugees in their own lousy lives, almost foreigners to themselves… They're Germans, they speak my language… It's better than nothing, to speak such a beautiful language, and they don't know how beautiful it is… In my theatre, they'll at least rediscover their own language…'

He started the car up again.

Not far from the Glienicke Bridge, there was a perfectly harmless routine identity control, carried out by a few Soviet soldiers. A Russian NCO translated what Brecht said from German into Russian and what he himself said from Russian into German. Maria couldn't help thinking that German sounded mean and ugly when translated into Russian and was transformed into the idiom of a prison warder. The inquisitorial gaze of a Soviet soldier inspecting the car's contents, and the meticulous care with which the NCO compared the Stayr's papers with the number-plate, instead of irritating Brecht, put him in a good mood, as if he felt protected by these soldier policemen. But for Maria Eich, this identity control reminded her of others, especially when her father, in the little Weiss theatre, had gone into his daughter's dressing room to tear off her little gold chain and the cross dangling from it.

He had returned to their big villa in Bad Voslau at around half past midnight and searched Maria's bedroom, throwing the mattresses upside down, flinging the contents of the chest of drawers onto the carpet, in a fit of hysteria, looking for a Bible, and the hardback volumes of Heine's lyric poems. He was yelling that he'd had it up to here with a 'Ca... Ca... Ca... tholic' daughter, who was exactly the same as her 'bigoted goose of a mother', then he had pressed Maria's face between his hands. He had made her look at herself in the mirror and asked her what she most looked like – a saint or a whore? Then, with a great dramatic gesture, he had chucked a missal and a tiny rosary down the toilet and said that he would never agree to his daughter living on her knees mumbling parables in which the human race was viewed as a herd of bleating cretins ready to be led to the abattoir.

Yes, while the Russians checked their papers, taking their time over it, Maria was thinking of that fit of paternal hysteria, of the calendar hanging near the hood of the chimney, over the old radiator, with the Catholic feast days furiously crossed out in thick red crayon.

She was thinking of her father who'd wanted to suppress everything that reminded him of the world of women, of the Bible commandments, of appeals to virtue and goodness. When the car started off again, Brecht asked Maria if she fancied a game of chess. She didn't fancy it in the slightest. She was still reliving her father's wild outburst, the two hours she had spent weeping in the bathroom, as if all the sweetness and solidity of the world had vanished along with the things he had flushed down the toilet.

6

Sometimes, after the rehearsals for *Antigone*, Brecht would go for a walk to the Märkisches Museum to stretch his legs. He observed the transformations of the park he was crossing, the young, acidic green foliage, the shady pathways, the broken branches. He told himself that the transformation of society ought to be an act as joyous as the transformation of nature in every season.

He remembered the road he used to love, in Svendborg, in the south of Denmark, with its disjointed cement surface, leading to a beach swept smooth by the wind, and the enigmatic question of the beauty of the dunes. The very first years of exile, between 1933 and 1939.

He would take shelter in a hollow and chew on a blade of grass. A cloud came along and turned a patch of sea purple; there was the distant hum of a coach, then a slow procession of more clouds from the Baltic; young butterflies merrily fluttered and twirled among the gorse bushes. Seagulls were mewling around a cluster of feathers scattered by the wind. The sky, now clear and growing vaster, signalled a change in the weather...

He remembered the first months of exile, in Denmark. They had been marked by two happy events: the purchase of a pretty house with a thatched roof, opposite the beach in the village of Skovsbostrand; and, above all, the fact that this was the year he had got to know the flamboyant Ruth Berlau, the wife of a rich industrialist from Copenhagen who had founded a Communist theatre for the workers. It was a time of evenings among the pine trees, shrieking children, raised glasses, the long oak table out on the grass, the 'fraternal peoples', the artist friends who had returned from Moscow, the drinking songs. On the sands of Skovsbostrand, he had sung along to the guitar, drunk a schnapps at the foot of a plum tree, lifted up the dress of that magnificent brunette and casually tugged the elastic straps of her bra.

Helene Weigel was stewing the plums and busying herself baking cakes, forgetting the presence of Ruth. Brecht pushed her gently up against a tree trunk. In the odour of resin, they made love. Then, they chatted. What about? Hitler and his gang. In Berlin, people were talking of peace, but you had only to see the smoke belching from the chimneys of the Krupp foundries, the thousands of tons of concrete being poured out in the middle of fields to form the auto-bahns, and the workshops where the wings of Stukas were being assembled, to know that it was going to be a long war, on a par with the literary courage of Brecht who, every morning, next to a roaring stove, blackened sheets of paper. He was composing poem-tracts, inventing German songs as he strummed his guitar.

Faced with this war, Brecht's energetic spirit, his comical expressions, his sexual hunger, his way of making the mattresses creak between two swims, his black leather jacket, his grey shirt, his excursions by car through the vast pastures along the sea, all made him a hero.

Hitler issued proclamations, frothed and foamed at the mouth, made his whole people march in goosestep, faster and faster: Brecht banged away at his rattling typewriter. Machine-gun poems. Finally, the great battle had come. The great, the entirely new, the never-before-heard-of way of making the German language squeal loud enough to stop the parades, the jackbooted processions, the banners and the Nazi slogans bellowed out into the silence of the stadiums.

Brecht, early in the morning, soaping himself, stripped to the waist, told Ruth Berlau how to get the working class to unite against 'that gang of criminals'.

In the afternoon, photos taken on the flight of steps, in the car, near the plum tree, in front of the garden table. Ruth Berlau walked on her stiletto heels into the master's office, while, outside, Helene Weigel cleared away the plates. His prowler's cap pulled over the corner of his face, with his ugly yobbo's mug and his ardent words, Brecht would talk. Brecht used to piss on the embers in a corner of the garden. He would extinguish Nazism the way he put out these embers, just by opening his flies. That was the kind of declaration he liked to make in front of his women. They were caught between amusement, stupor, and disquiet, and wondered whether Nazism wasn't his one big chance, the opportunity he had been waiting for to demonstrate the full measure of his intelligence.

Often, in the evenings, he would really let his hair down. He burst out laughing, and showered his guests and his family with caustic remarks. His eyes pierced through his audience, his voice was expressionless as he read appeals, speeches on behalf of the working class, a never-ending text on the need for propaganda; he vociferously attempted to drown out the holy mass being celebrated by the Nazis. Later on, he would slip behind the house, and steal through a hole in the hedge to join Ruth Berlau. She would be waiting for him in the car, her blouse unbuttoned.

Wouldn't Hitler, whom he called 'the house painter', and his gang of weirdoes all be swept away by the earthly, expansive joy, the gunpowder and explosive force of his poems? He threw his typewritten speeches over the thatched roof of his house; they scattered in the wind, and were borne away by the long calm clouds of the Baltic to the Soviet Union.

The brown plague would be driven away by the wind of his inspiration. It was perfectly simple, implacable, obvious.

When he came back into the huge icy villa at Weissensee, he could hear Maria. She was tidying away the clothes and then, as silence fell, he would half-open the door. Maria was asleep, or pretending to be asleep.

Brecht would make himself a herbal tea in the kitchen. He went back into his bedroom where the air was colder. He stretched out on the blankets. The curtain embroidered with tassels, the marble mantelpiece, the sets of proofs of his plays, his notes on *Antigone* and Kleist's *Broken Jug*, the notebooks, the sharpened pencils. All those notes that Maria had carefully and surreptitiously photographed for Hans Trow.

The light from the little lamp, brilliantly reflected on the white gloss bedpost. The heavy, deep tolling of a church bell, reminding him that Skovsbostrand was a peninsula and still imbued, irrevocably, with theological seriousness...

Sometimes, Maria would knock on the double door, or rather it was a sort of scratching. The camera, a Zirko that Maria used when she spied on Brecht, stayed hidden under the woollens in a suitcase.

7

Ever since the incredible success of *Mother Courage*, in January 1949, Theo Pilla had been entrusted by Hans Trow with the task of keeping a particularly close eye on the Seagull, the Soviet-German club that also provided a location for the offices of Helene Weigel. Theo Pilla, quite casually (as he thought), would question the waitresses, the cooks, the painters and even the locksmith who oiled the new locks on Helene Weigel's study door. He asked his questions bluntly, pocketed the sugar lumps that were lying around, and demanded that the plumber siphon a washbasin because he thought he'd seen Maria getting rid of some notes hastily scrawled on toilet paper.

Everyone noticed his bluntness and mistrusted this dark, stocky, agile little man, who scared the least little housewife with the threat that he would 'reveal her Nazi past to the People's Tribunal'.

Hans was amused by this son of a cork seller from the Black Forest who had spent half the war in a submarine patrolling the Atlantic – in the ships' galley. Theo had no sense for the mystique of politics, but having been an apprentice cook in his teens, he had shown a remarkable sense for denunciation. In him, it was an illness: he mistrusted everyone, imagined similarities between completely unconnected details and, under cover of 'class justice', treated all and sundry with a congenital, absurd, quite unexpected mistrust. But, curiously enough, he could draw up reports that were admirable in their technical precision, inadvertently providing Hans Trow with evidence that meant he had enough proof to close the files on a great number of affairs.

Theo Pilla had taken a sudden dislike to theatre actors, especially the ones who were popular; they found everything amusing, liked to talk dirty and, quite evidently, did not suffer from hunger as did the rest of the population.

For his part, Theo Pilla would, between two surveillance sessions, stick a fork into a pie or a few cabbage leaves left at the bottom of a saucepan, as soon as the cooks in the Seagull Club had their backs turned. In this way he would haul his podgy figure around, either to dip his finger into the gravy, or to hover behind a partition, pretending to read the paper, while listening to what was being said at the neighbouring table. He noted down everything said by Ruth Berlau about Brecht's plan to put on *The Private Tutor* by Lenz, with a good part for Maria. She also mentioned Vladimir Semyonov, the Soviet commander in the zone, who had been so thrilled by Weigel's acting in *Mother Courage* that he had decided to raise her overall salary and her individual fee for each performance. Theo Pilla also knew that Semyonov had signed, with his own chubby hand, a document authorising an increase in the Berliner Ensemble's grant for running costs.

On coming out of Luisenstrasse, Pilla had returned to the offices in Schumannstrasse. From there, he had gone to the hall of the former imperial theatre to find Hans Trow. He had confided to him, mysteriously, that 'the little goldcrest Brecht would become the imperial eagle of the regime'. Hans Trow continued to leaf through *Neues Deutschland* as he asked Pilla what the hell he was driving at with his bird stories. He didn't give a damn whether Brecht was a bullfinch, a chaffinch or a goldfinch.

Yet again, Hans Trow realised that Theo Pilla filled the air around him with a sickly sweet kitchen smell. The biggest drawback of an intelligence service lies in having to choose complete idiots in the belief that they are closer to the majority of people, because they think and act like the most stupid. That's how a system collapses, thought Hans. A good Prussian doesn't condescend to work with the son of a cork seller from the Black Forest. Still, he continued to smile, and muttered his thanks so as not to discourage his assistant, or – worse – stifle his natural enthusiasm for denunciation.

That evening, in the entrance hall of the old imperial theatre, there were a lot of children, a few workers near the grand staircase, and above all, bureaucrats. They all look alike: dressed in dark clothes, ill-fitting coats. The sort of people who spend their time granting or obtaining permission, all the bureaucracy that lives parasitically off artistic work. They look like professors. They talk about the abuse of mercantilism and how the working classes have such a liking for pure smut. Men with square jaws and a military haircut, petty-bourgeois women whose eyes open wide at the sight of imperial gilding: they come here to regenerate themselves. Slowly they climb the staircase, leaving the traces of their damp soles on the carpet. Their clothes haven't been ironed properly; they exchange remarks on the deficiencies of the food distribution system.

Hans Trow returned, holding his tickets. They had seats in the eighth row, on the side. Hans recognised the plump Hella Wuolijoki who had welcomed Brecht to her Finnish estate. A big round face, a great tress of blond hair twisted round the top of her head, a fur round her neck; she was forever leaning out of her seat in the circle to see who was the man wearing a red shirt down there, in the first row. It was the actor Leonard Steckel, the one who would soon be playing the role of Puntila, the play that Brecht himself had written at her home and with her help...

Hans Trow let Theo Pilla by so he could take his seat. Hans himself took the foldaway seat, which creaked. The lights went down, as did the hubbub of chatter. The light onstage revealed a lunar landscape. A moor. Mother Courage's cart. And buckets and kitchen implements rattling together.

'That's not how you make an entrance!' said Theo in a low voice. 'It's bloody stupid!...'

'Shut up...'

Two and a half hours later, they emerged from the Deutsches Theater, while numerous groups stood chattering on the pavement.

'She looks graceful on stage,' said Theo Pilla, 'you'd say she was a seventeen-year-old girl. A teenager.'

He was talking about Maria Eich.

Hans Trow lit a small cigar. He was wondering what difference there was between an actress, a prostitute, a banker's daughter and a primary-school teacher. Maria's face, with its stage make-up, had disturbed him. He wondered whether actors ended up being corrupted by the fees they were paid, the gifts, the medals, the compliments, the admirers. Those actors got invited everywhere, like children at Christmas. He remembered that one of them had shot himself in the mouth during the rehearsals for *Mother Courage* in Munich. Theo Pilla said, 'This Berliner Ensemble is a real loony bin...'

Taking shelter in his ironic private thoughts, Hans said nothing and watched the smoke rise from his small cigar.

'The way they take a bow,' continued Theo Pilla, 'when they come back at the end, to the front of the stage...'

'Yes...'

'They bow, bent double, with their grease-paint still on, disfigured... a loony bin... They look like puppets... sick people...'

'Ah... Really?' said Hans who enjoyed watching Pilla get swept away by his frenzied, whimsical reflections, which led nowhere.

'Don't you think so?'

'No.'

'They take a bow, holding hands… The footlights are in front of them, it's as if there was snow lighting them up. A loony bin – full of ghosts. They hold hands, come forward and go backward, and come forward again and smile at each other and smile at us… a loony bin… they're all mad…'

'And we are sick,' said Hans with a smile.

Later on, an immense river of clouds was gently drifting towards the Reichstag.

'She looked very good – Maria, with the recruiting officer,' said Theo.

'Very good,' said Hans.

'High-spirited, at ease…'

'Very…'

Theo started to sniff.

'You smell of wood… springtime wood…'

'Yes.'

'The odour of undergrowth… my whole child-hood…'

Theo continued, 'When they bend double to take a bow, they look like dead puppets… Or am I wrong?'

'No, you're not wrong,' said Hans.

'Puppets, with their make-up on, in the spotlights, playing the parts of peasants, adjutants, tarts… there you have it, the whole of German theatre,' said Theo.

Hans placed his hand on Theo's shoulder. Theo was getting carried away.

'Shut up.'

They listened. There was a low, regular squeaking noise coming from behind an old fairground stall in front of a clump of birches. It was just an iron swing, creaking in the wind. Rusty rings squeaking on an axle.

Theo continued, 'When I was a kid' (Hans hated it when he said 'kid'), 'when I was a kid, my father took me to see Schiller's *Wallenstein*. It was in the annex of my school. *Wallenstein* was already nothing but camp followers, adjutants' stories, military camps, emperors, soldiers, drums and flutes, plenty of nosh, hanged men, grub and hanged men, German theatre, is that all there is to it? Tables, soldiers, whores, camp followers. Schiller already... that's all there is to theatre then? Orphans, hanged men. A pewter jug, recruiting officers who go round tickling whores' bums? That's what German theatre has been for centuries... Bloody hell...'

'No,' said Hans, 'that's not it...'

Hans had for some time already been walking along without paying too much attention to Theo's chattering. That unstoppable blah-blah-blah reminded him of the chore of having to peel potatoes outside his parents' home in Wittenberg. The cook, Lisbeth, had used this as an opportunity to pour out onto little Hans everything that went through her head. Peeling potatoes inspired her gift for fantasy. She would foretell the future of the world, dream of enormous machines yet to come that would peel potatoes, carrots, turnips; the whole people would be liberated from the chore of peeling vegetables. Then she waxed even more prophetic: chickens would be plucked automatically, poultry gutted on the assembly belt, and the domestic calm of the Trow household would be safe from all famine forever and ever, amen!

Basically, Pilla, just like the Trows' cook, let himself be swept aloft by his imagination, like the self-taught man he was. His wealth of declarations, often undistinguished, his interminable, labyrinthine hypotheses resembled those potato peelings that had piled up in the old newspapers. Hans' father, on the other hand, absorbed night and day in juridical paperwork, sitting in his huge office overlooking fields of potatoes, had lost his power of speech at university. It was exactly as if the gothic brickwork of the libraries had made him mute, melancholy, with a bottomless melancholia. Hans' father had fallen back on secret ruminations, and become hostile to ordinary human communication. He only ever uttered a few paltry, measured words at the family table. He made Hans, the youngest in the family, recite the series of dates of the Thirty Years' War.

Hans remembered his father's long silences, sometimes solemn, at other times sombre, as if they were a way of rebuking the family for its existence. The few bursts of laughter came from the kitchen. The table, the chairs, the stove, the spectral white sun on the bare fields spoke more expressively to this father of his. He would eat his soup cold and the only thing he could stand in literature was the forest twilight of the *Song of the Nibelungs*. He imposed on the whole estate the atmosphere of a criminal court at the moment sentence is passed.

Hans had always wondered how his father had gone so far as to take off his trousers and give his wife three children. This father, who was always putting off any discussion, would gaze out, through the window, at the potato fields of Mecklenburg. Could he already see an SA patrol marching up the great oak staircase and tramping with its boots over the parquet floor of the corridor, entering his office without knocking and taking down, among other things, the great painting of the *Last Judgement* that was hanging between two chests of drawers? His gaze fixed on the lines of poplars, could he read on the horizon the disasters of the Third Reich? Could he see in the sky the dozens of Stukas roaring up into the clouds, their fuselages gleaming with steel? Could he see all of his son Hans' lead soldiers falling in the snow of Stalingrad? Could he guess at the sickly-sweet hell of the secret services? Hundreds of shelves lining the corridors, the cast-iron management of mankind's deeds and exploits, the frenzied quest for ideological betrayal, the restless, diabolical rummaging through the dunghill of reports that focused less on political groups... This is what preoccupied Hans Trow while Theo Pilla babbled endlessly on.

He was talking about those 'conceited actors whose performances were a load of old cobblers'.

'Do you realise,' said Theo, 'do you realise that from Schiller to Brecht, nothing's changed? We're in the same old military camp... the same Thirty Years' War? With the same recruiting officers, the same whores...'

'I suppose so,' said Hans with a smile, sinking down onto a bench.

Hans pulled out the theatre tickets, tore them up and scattered the bits onto the snow.

'Pewter jugs, and men giving camp followers a slap on the arse... theatre is the art of chaos gazing at the art of order... don't you think so, Hans?'

'No, I don't.'

Theo Pilla took off his scarf, opened his collar, brushed the snow off his coat, and continued, 'Getting dressed, getting undressed, telling lies, putting on your make-up, taking off your make-up, telling lies. Getting undressed, taking off your make-up, talking, reciting, declaiming, taking off your make-up, always repeating the same stupid phrase... that's really something. Coming to take your bow like macabre puppets trying to scare the people in the front row with the light shining up on you from the footlights... what do you think of it all? Is *that* a life? Actors scare people...'

'They make them laugh too,' said Hans.

'Oh yeah? Scaring people? Making them laugh? Taking a bow, making them laugh, scaring them, do you think that's a life?... It's a big con; they must get everything mixed up – making people laugh, telling lies, producing prose and poetry, their thoughts, their words. Where's their private life? They must get it all muddled, surely?...'

'Brecht doesn't muddle things, believe me...'

'But what about Maria? Our Maria?...'

'I don't know,' said Hans, who had placed his cigar stub on one of the bench's wooden strips.

'They must keep getting tied up in knots; they must scare themselves and make themselves laugh without knowing how or why... Don't you agree, Hans?'

'No,' said Hans, blowing on the embers of his cigar. 'Perhaps... well...'

'They're all a load of touts,' added Theo.

He rose and shook his coat.

'Personally speaking, I'd bung them all in the nick. We just don't need them... To think we're here for *them*...'

Later on, when Pilla had finished grousing, and Hans had stopped being evasive, the two men got up, the minutes went by; they walked towards the Spree, which is a little broader just here.

8

On the days when Brecht hadn't included Maria Eich's name on the cast list for the rehearsals for *Antigone*, she would go into the American Sector. Thanks to the pass crossed in red that Hans Trow had ensured she got, she could join her daughter Lotte. The trams were full, there were barges in single file on the Spree, trucks filed with potatoes, plumes of black smoke from the factory chimneys, deaf-mutes selling Bibles, widows hawking around the patent-leather shoes of their dear departed, the cries of a newspaper vendor with a few sweets for sale: this was the Berlin that moved by her, in its gaudy colours, silver-hued.

Maria took several trams that crossed the Steglitz district, then Lichterfelder in the direction of Wannsee. Ramifications of shadows along the endless brick walls of former barracks, woods of ash trees abandoned to the rabbit warrens, woodland pines and cimbro pines creating a silence on the approaches to Wannsee.

Maria would get out of the tram, and walk quickly across patches of sandy ground and past overgrown villas. She went round an old swimming pool filled with brackish water, and heard a frog jumping into it with a plop, while, on the steps, a few lizards warmed themselves on the stones, when it was sunny.

Maria's mother, Lena Zorn, who looked after Lotte, lived in a huge dirty-yellow villa with a sand-covered peristyle that had birds' nests in its corners.

The only thing that seemed alive, around this building with its flaking shutters, was the grass in the field and its run-to-seed plants, its lilacs.

Inside the villa, the living room resembled a railway compartment with its heavy fabric wall coverings, seats taken straight out of the Bundesbahn, its bull's-eye windows and a whole set of pewter dish-ware piled on top of a Bismarck-style sideboard. Grandmother hovered around in a grey dress. Over her shoulders was a blackish fringed shawl, and around her, glasses of whisky. She kept her purse with her wherever she went. She cursed the price of penicillin. She would get up from her seat only to call Lotte, who was playing outside.

Mother and daughter spoke little. They avoided bringing up the past. 'Oh yes! Oh yes!' Lena kept saying to her daughter, 'you're perfectly right, just you join the winning side! I know you're a first-rate anti-fascist! I know! Anti-fascist right from the start! Neither your father nor your husband had noticed as much! Neither had I!...' She sighed, and let her hands (the left one still holding her purse) sink onto her thighs, as if she were exhausted by this declaration, then she remained with her back glued to the leather of her seat, motionless, as if the mill wheel of her memories had stopped on 8th May 1945 at eight o'clock in the morning, when she had heard that Nazi Germany had unconditionally surrendered.

Ever since then, she had been bringing up Lotte. She took care of her asthma, and kept counting and recounting her crumpled banknotes. From where they were lodged away in her purse, she would sometimes pull out, as documents of bygone time, old photographs of Vienna.

Then there was a morose cup of tea, and pretzels as hard as stone. In the gloom, a chandelier wrapped in a parachute sheet hung, menacingly, like a ghost, over the table… A neighbour, all pink and glowing, appeared, a plump figure, wrapped in frills and flounces; she began to smother the little girl with kisses, hugging her close, burying her in excessive display of affection. While the tea was being poured, silence.

'How are her asthma attacks?' asked Maria.

'She doesn't have them when she's with me,' her mother replied.

A sense of awkwardness set in. Maria's gaze wandered round the knick-knacks and the china arranged on a shelf. Her eyes lingered on an old photograph, in its frame of tarnished silver: two mocking faces, that of Maria and that of her husband with his forage cap and his hair cut very short. Maria said to herself that there had been a bright, carefree period; now, everything was dark and inexplicable and oppressive.

'You're working with that man Brecht?…'

'Yes.'

'I thought that fellow was dead!' the neighbour exclaimed in astonishment.

'No, he isn't dead.'

'He fled the country ages ago... A Communist...'

The conversation would falter again. Everyone got up. The neighbour said, 'I know one little girl who won't be late to bed tonight...'

On the steps outside, Maria's eyes sought out her daughter. The girl was playing in her corner. Lotte's loneliness was obvious. Maria went over to the child, kissed her, and walked away, leaving the house.

Ten minutes later, Maria found herself back in a screeching, rattling tram, feeling dispossessed and overwhelmed by grief. She was becoming a foreigner to herself.

Then she would take refuge in a white, arched café in Würmlingerstrasse. The earthenware stove roared and glowed. There was a heavy round oaken table... a glass of beer that foamed and then stopped foaming... The peace and silence of this place enabled her to calm down. Her head nodded, she dozed off.

The café proprietor would sometimes slip another log into the stove and gaze at this pretty young woman as she slept.

In her dream, Maria was playing in the woods round Vienna. She was gathering flowers, then she slipped off into the undergrowth. She was attacked by wasps, and stung. The wasps vanished in gluey swarms beneath her blouse.

When she came out, Maria was in a daze: people were talking, cars were passing, coats were walking round. She leant against the railings. The yellow sun of evening calmed her down.

9

At the end of November 1950, during the last rehearsals for *Antigone*, Maria Eich noticed that the Cultural Services were making more and more telephone calls and visits to the actors, and asking them more and more questions. She had the feeling that there must be some pretty odd reports doing the rounds in the Ministry.

The clamorous door bell was forever interrupting the rehearsals, or the telephone tinkling at the foot of the stairs in the Weissensee villa. One Sunday morning, in the rehearsal hall in Reinhardtstrasse, a bureaucrat paid them a visit. He interrupted the exercise, dispelled the cheerful atmosphere that Brecht had created. And those who were busy limbering up (a slow pirouette facing the hall, feet nimble, legs stretched out, arms in a circle, then lowered to the sides) continued to work, but glanced sidelong at the curious visitor.

The member of the Cultural Commission kept his hat in his hand; he was wearing a shabby gabardine, and had a thick neck. He ostentatiously closed the piano lid and pushed away the scores by Dessau. Then he smiled, the way a spy smiles, which meant – as Brecht knew – a report landing on Dymschitz's desk, with a copy to the Cultural League: a convoluted, tortuous piece of red tape, denouncing the aestheticist and formalist drift of the Berliner Ensemble company, its elitism, its jargon. In it, Brecht was presented as a casual artist mumbling fables and providing disconcerting examples of insolence. It was repeated for the umpteenth time that the Department of Cultural Affairs expected 'solid proletarian art', art that would be healthy and useful like a good saucepan, like a wheelbarrow, like a hammer. But Brecht was always dressing things up, drawing deductions, holding forth, expressing opinions, saying anything and then its opposite on the pretext that this was dialectics. This slippery eel of a man gave the impression of playing sly tricks with everyone, male and female. In some people he encouraged a superiority complex. He was forever uttering ironic remarks, he spoke out loud and strong, ridiculed the psychological discussions that the actors demanded, and at every turn quoted Shakespeare, with whom he obsessively identified. In short, a wily customer, with a knack for casting derision on the plays in the repertoire, explaining that it is through sacrilege that great works are preserved, and not through some 'dry-as-dust veneration'.

Maria realised that the ministry's desks were sagging under the weight of reports inspired by jealous writers, eminent members of the Cultural League. She herself sometimes gave up the attempt to follow Brecht – she found some of his lectures on Greek theatre stupefyingly dull, as on the day when he went on and on about the difference between the hatred of Achilles for Hector and the hatred of a worker for his boss.

In the evening, the tone changed: it was always the same. He hoicked off Maria's pullover, and tore her skirt off her.

Then she felt as humiliated as if she were undergoing a medical inspection.

Afterwards, she dissolved some pills in a glass of water. The master had heart problems.

One Tuesday evening, Brecht and Maria both attended a meeting of the Writers' Union. There was a big crowd. Helene Weigel came up behind Brecht and murmured, 'Anyone would think Maria Eich had faded into thin air. She comes along, vanishes, disappears, comes back; she's a ghost, that little protégée of yours, you're living with a ghost. I hope your memory will be good enough to remember where you've put her, good enough to know where your charming little breath of air has gone.'

'Don't you like her?' said Brecht, sticking a gherkin into his sandwich with a fork.

He added, 'Someone's already made the same remark to me.'

'What remark?'

'That Maria behaves like a breath of air and that one day she'll disappear.'

Brecht filled his plate with calf's-head terrine, with its fragments of cartilage that crackle between your teeth; he wished he was in his pyjamas, back in the huge tiled kitchen in the Weissensee villa, watching the hair of Ruth Berlau shimmering on her shoulders... Oh, not the old woman she was now, but the young Swedish girl of 1941, with her red-and-white check swimming costume, and her exuberance when she went for a swim in the Baltic. Maria was an interesting girl, but not as good as Ruth...

Some people came up to him.

Brecht put down his plate and lit a cigar. He was drawn over towards the centre of the room. He wondered whether his astrological sign met with Moscow's approval. Over there, Nero held sway...

He replied with humour, and even wit, to the toasts they proposed. He did so especially for Helene, who had become a popular and successful character. He didn't want to 'mess things up' for her, as he put it, nor to cause her any anxiety, but the news from Moscow really wasn't very good. There was a storm brewing. He'd ask his designer to take a brush loaded with black China ink and add a long line to the stage set. Just like that, deftly: a signature.

One day, he'd go to China. A valley in the mountains. A tiny house, the clatter of his typewriter, the fog in the ravines visible from the kitchen, the cock crowing. From time to time, a little grunt, quite unmalicious, as he read the newspapers from Germany. He would draw a chalk circle and in it he would set two cocks and a child, and then he would watch; he'd button up his jacket. At the start of the afternoon, a siesta, veal kidneys, a few cuts to an over-long poem, then a visit to the workshop of a Chinese woodworker. He'd walk through the wood shavings. He'd try out his new desk, a table made of light wood. A dog's paws, sparrows, curtains, a stool, terrine, a beer. Poems in China ink…

In the summer, he would wash himself in an enamel pot. Dip a finger in a jam jar to taste the jam. Gooseberries, fatigue, sleep, gossip. He'd whistle to his dog then come to play jacks with the woodworker's son. All evening long, he would yawn in the courtyard as he gazed at the spindle trees drawn in the fog. He would smoke a cigar.

This is what he was thinking while the boss of the Moscow Academy, Sergey something-or-other, held his hand, wrapped it within his own, waxing lyrical about the Free German Youth…

An old friend, a certain Rudolf Prestel, a self-styled comrade from school days in Augsburg, came over with his plate of beef in gravy and whispered, 'Grub first! Ethics after… Hey, Bertolt!… Hey?…'

Langhoff and Dymschitz, with their well-cut suits, resembled notaries. Their wives were wearing awful dresses. There were also, in a corner of the room, Arnold Zweig and Johannes Becher, who had had the honour of seeing their prose flung into the bonfire by rosy-cheeked SA men, while the poems were consumed on a cobbled square surrounded by Brown-shirts…

The other man came over, the childhood friend, and said, 'Here, it's ethics first! Grub after…' as he waved his fork at the contents of his plate.

Whereupon, Brecht started to pretend that he had

been called over by a group of young people, and he put on a playful act. He seized a female student by the shoulder.

'Stay in character! Smile! I'll find you a part in *Puntila*! Brecht's word of honour!...'

Before the girl could reply, the master had slipped two fingers behind Maria's back to tickle her. 'Grub first, ethics after,' he whispered. He was suddenly overwhelmed by an indefinable feeling at the sight of this provincial society, this eddy of grey clothes... They had the academic stiffness of the new bureaucracy in Moscow...

He refused to say any more, slipped into his coat, and walked out to the official car. To cut himself off from the world and lie down in the maelstrom of nothingness. Then he thought better of it: the world is in ruins and starving, how can I complain about being here?

The driver asked him what time he was to pick him up the next day. At half past seven!... Then, on his bed, he stretched out and listened to a 78 rpm, a Bruno Walter recording that Paul Dessau had given him.

10

Five days after the start of the dress rehearsal, Brecht went up to Maria's dressing room. She was washing her underwear in the little washbasin. He prowled round her, then sat in a crimson velvet armchair framed in baroque gilt.

'You're not light enough, Maria.'

Maria was soaping her bra.

'Could you do me a favour?'

Maria thought he meant a sexual favour.

But Brecht continued, 'Could you be a bit lighter? I've been thinking,' he went on, 'that if you waved your arms about less, you'd be lighter.'

'Yes, of course.'

Silence.

'You know what I mean?'

Brecht lit a cigar and, as always when he felt awkward, wrapped himself in a cloud of smoke and assumed a mocking, artificial air.

'Could you pass me the towel?' Maria asked.

Brecht handed over the towel.

'Be lighter… like this smoke… lighter…'

Maria held her underwear up to examine it, and started to hang it out on the iron wire stretched from the screen to the hat stand.

'Cut down a bit,' murmured Brecht, 'don't you think?'

'I knew what you meant.'

There was a silence.

'You shouldn't take it like that.'

'Sorry.'

Brecht rotated his cigar to drop the ash into the tin plate that acted as an ashtray.

'Someone's already made the same remark to me,' she said.

'Who?'

'Helene Weigel.'

'Are you sure?'

'Absolutely!'

Brecht was hungry, had a craving for bacon. Maria was slipping into her blood-red ratteen skirt. As her zip had got stuck, Brecht rose to help her do it up.

'You've put on weight!'

'No,' she said.

She was buttoning up her blouse when she noticed that a mother-of-pearl button was coming loose. She tugged at the thread and the button fell onto the chair, bounced, and rolled under Brecht's armchair. He bent down vaguely to see where it had gone.

Maria went down on all fours to look for it.

'Do you want me to help you?…'

'No, thanks. I can do it.'

'You don't want me to call a dresser?'

'No thank you.'

There was a silence.

'I'm joking. Forgive me,' said Brecht.

He reflected that he ought to add a long brush-stroke in black to the stage backdrop, a long piece of beige cotton canvas. Maria sewed the button back on, standing there pulling nervously at the needle and thread.

Finally, she snapped the thread off with her teeth, finished buttoning her blouse and looked at Brecht as he put out his cigar, crushing it obstinately. Brecht had aged. His lower lip was drooping a bit. It was flabby. He'd forgotten to shave a corner under his left ear.

'I'm sorry for what I just said.'

'You didn't say anything,' she replied.

'Yes I did, I said that…'

'I know what you said…'

Brecht thought, 'The actor's delightful poison.' Then, his desire for reconciliation with her suddenly turned to hatred: who did this bloody stupid cow think she was?

Maria had put on a jacket and asked, 'Can you get my lines for me?'

Brecht got up, opened the wardrobe and took the script from off the shelf. Maria opened it at the page marked by a postcard from Bad-Voslau that her father had sent her while on holiday in that Austrian spa; she'd been eight. She read her lines, underlined certain passages. Brecht started to examine her. Sometimes he would glance sidelong at her, and tell himself that a curious sense of solitude emanated from her, something characteristic of children abandoned for years on end in a boarding school. This solitude gave her a halo of mystery, a presence-absence that was so bizarre that you came to the conclusion that Maria Eich was deprived of destiny, that she lived one single, eternal day. If she had indeed trodden the boards, if she had condescended to show her figure on a theatre stage, it was clearly to exhibit that single, monotonous day in which she had been living ever since her adolescence. In this way, actors resemble convalescents taking good care of themselves, as if all the important things had vanished when they lost their health and as if, ever since emerging from their boarding schools, their years of isolation, they can never recover the health they remember enjoying in childhood. 'Yes,' Brecht said to himself, 'no more destiny; this woman is merely a travelling bag placed on a theatre stage.'

On the nights before her meetings with Hans Trow, Maria Eich always slept badly. She had switched the radio on quietly and learnt that there'd been an unpleasant exchange of diplomatic notes between Stalin and the West. In the morning, she'd tried to wake herself up with a cup of strong tea, then she had gone to the rehearsal for *Antigone*. Since there weren't any scenes in which she was directly involved, she had settled down in the eighth row, among the empty seats. Brecht, who had been in the middle of giving his actors some advice, suddenly stopped and came straight up to Maria as she rummaged in her bag looking for a bracelet.

He murmured, all in one go as if he hadn't had time to draw breath, 'Most people aren't aware, Maria, of the consequences that art can have on them, of the consequences good and bad. Representation gives us an image of the world, a clear or muddled image of the world, you should know that and, if you don't pay close attention, that image will leave no one intact, not even you! Art which is not considered, understood and contemplated degrades you! Can you get that into your head?'

Then, he had bizarrely pulled down the collar of Maria's jacket as if in some puritanical gesture to conceal the actress' breasts. He climbed back on stage.

The actors were waiting, wondering what was happening in the darkness of the auditorium. They could see from Brecht's impassive face, his cold expression, that he was in a foul mood... The scene continued. The posts and the horses' skulls and the work table had been metamorphosed into incongruous objects floating around in a dingy light. The fact that a spotlight short-circuited didn't exactly help.

At the beginning of the afternoon, Maria went for a walk in the park. She was struck by the place's solitude. Near the pine trees, there was a cinema, the Metropole, with a broad yellow glass awning covered in snow. She sat on the steps after slipping a copy of the *Berliner Tagblatt* under her bottom, and forgot her bad mood as she watched soldiers in great-coats endlessly chatting and stamping their feet to keep warm. The sky took on every appearance of a kitsch sunset with its red streaks over the ruins. Maria felt calmer. She got up and made her way to the address given by Hans Trow. She arrived some ten minutes early.

The Swan Tavern was low and vaulted, and had small, round, high windows with little pieces of coloured glass. Heavy rectangular tables in dark wood. Near the window, in a cloud of blue smoke, an extremely elegant young man was leafing through a notebook and would occasionally shift a piece of tracing paper as he measured something with a small rule. Maria had ordered a tea and sat waiting in the half-light.

Hans Trow arrived. They talked about Brecht and the Berliner Ensemble, whose sign was now swinging, round like a Mercedes sign, over the Deutsches Theater. Maria felt liberated and let the words run away with her. She knew she was being listened to. She reflected, 'No one listens to me the way he does'. She wondered whether her secret information was favourably received and studied by the intelligence services.

Hans told her that he'd known a good theatre in Stettin before the war, where officers, friends of his, would often go. There was a gap in the conversation, a silence, but something fresh and calm linked them together. Everything seemed clear, tranquil, familiar, in a way that it hadn't been for years. She felt like talking to him more familiarly, calling him 'du'. Then Hans placed a cold, metallic object in her hand. It was a tiny Kodak camera, imported from the West. 'I have the feeling they're watching us. They're all watching us,' she said, as Hans paid.

They took a few steps and Maria didn't know what to do, what to say. She noticed that the evening gives a curious clear outline to certain ruins. They carried on walking, and stepped over a fence. All her actions, the quarrels with Brecht, the misunderstandings, were part of an ancient world that was dying. Without altogether grasping what was sweeping over her, Maria felt a sense of trust, certainty, the need to confess that a particular grace had overwhelmed her, a sense of lightness. She yearned for a hot, bright café, a whole day to walk down a pavement that would lead straight on, out of Berlin. She could see a church dome and a plane coming in to land at Tegel.

At what moment had she drifted away from this fresh, original world that always returned as soon as she was in Hans Trow's presence?

It was enough just to be walking at his side. She had just to hear him explaining how to use the Kodak, and all her doubts, anxieties, bad dreams, shadows and fears vanished; he had just to speak quietly, and the human race, all at once, no longer seemed to be made of lead. Why was there a sudden sense of hopefulness and fun? Even this street seller, under the elevated railway, who, with his combs and his two bound volumes of Goethe, his trinkets and his piece of lace ribbon, was a messenger. Street sellers, sweet messengers... She'd need to think this through... Hans bought a comb.

Then, he spread out his mac between the black fir trees and started to talk.

He spoke of his mission as if he wanted to replay a certain part of his life that he had set aside, after some event that he kept secret. But the fatigue and disarray were evident on his face when he declared, with a sort of painful contempt, 'Now I know what I want!'

He had started speaking more loudly. And, beneath those fir trees, it was a strange and ambiguous message, this repeated phrase, 'I know what I want! Maria.'

They separated near the Deutsches Theater. The glowing emblem of the Berliner Ensemble swung in the evening, casting its reflection in the canal. Hans walked off along the bank. Maria said to herself, 'Everything is stagnant and torpid, dozing, the world is asleep'. A greenish, leaden-hued barge glided, deeply laden, through the water.

The next day, despite her good resolutions ('I must always appear playful, I am Antigone, I am light, I am an angel'), Maria started to feel panicky. Someone scratched at the door while she was showering. She repeated, 'Yes?… Yes?…'

And Brecht replied, 'Why don't you bolt the bathroom door? Are you expecting someone?'

Then she felt his fingers, the towel, as she was pushed towards the bed and then onto the carpet.

While he was embracing her, he murmured, 'Who for?'

He bit deeper. And Maria was taken aback by this bite.

'Who for? Who were you shaking your ass for this morning?'

The bedside lamp had fallen down.

He left her, slamming the door behind him. Maria felt she was a real 'Mistress Courage' – she had aroused his jealousy and sated his ardour in the middle of what he called his 'erotic thriller'. When he came back into the room, they were just a man and a woman, living together, moving around, speaking, apparently relaxed, though they had both lost their self-assurance. The words they exchanged were tone-less. A cigarette lighter flashed in the darkness. Mentally, he repeated to himself, 'The one woman takes, the other gives, the one gives, the other takes'.

He sat on the bed and opened an American novel. He didn't read, but reflected that with Ruth he slid onto the carpet, with Helli he did it on the stairs, with Greta, sitting on the iron grille round a clump of flowers. With Ruth he would stop the black Stayr and do it on the roadside bank, without even getting undressed.

12

The dress rehearsal for *Antigone* took place in April; although the play was granted the automatic homage of the official organs, they touched only in passing on Maria's performance. Master Brecht had fought against there being any idea of hierarchy in a company of actors.

May and June went by. There were moves and meetings. Preparations for the Festival of Youth. Maria had taken to sucking honey-flavoured pastilles, as her voice tired quickly. At the end of July, she left with Brecht and his gang for the Baltic coast.

Ahrenshoop. On a long strip of sand, a little town that was worth being preserved in a museum, with pretty narrow houses, sculptured woodwork, flights of steps, interior staircases, a sense of tranquillity dating from the start of the 19th century. Further on, the dunes, then the expanses of wet sand, then the breakwaters gnawed at by the sea water, a few bathing cabins, broad flat stretches. Plains of salty water...

Photographers came to take some pictures of Brecht.

Maria was put up in a family boarding house near a wooden church. Sometimes she would be invited to share an aperitif in the evening. The rest of the time, she strolled through the dunes. Bright days that give you the impression the earth has stopped turning. Rough, threadbare, angular children, with spindly limbs, shivering in the cold, dived into intensely green waves that beat all along the jetty. They wash everything, those waves, they oxidise everything, people's backs and knees, the seagulls' droppings and the buoys. Maria would dive into this cold water to forget.

She would go off and leave Brecht's troupe behind. Days of wind and light, long and perfect. The tides lull you to sleep, imposing themselves. Maria would sometimes stagger through the waves, watching the children and thinking of her daughter. Families stretched out on their bath towels left her feeling melancholy. She would forget her weariness by swimming obstinately.

In the afternoon, the sky's silence was pale blue. The bathers turned into tiny dots, the sea sparkled. Space, clouds... A certain divine sweetness filled Maria. The sea's forces seemed to swallow up the figures in the brilliant expanse of the open water. Maria wondered why anyone should wish to explain incomprehensible things by comprehensible things. She would sit on a bench admiring the long waves of the evening, coming in from the Scandinavian countries and making the coast foam white with such regularity.

One evening when they were together, while Maria was screwing her left eye and then her right eye as she gazed at a pine tree, Brecht asked her, 'So what are you playing at, Maria?'

'Oh, just keeping myself amused…'

The silence grew deeper and everyone turned to look at Maria.

'But…'

'I was measuring the difference between what you can see with your left eye and what you can see with your right eye.'

Helene Weigel came over to the table with an oil lamp and placed it between the cups and glasses.

'And?' asked Brecht.

'Oh, nothing.'

She added, 'I was wondering what the explanation for Evil is… and if there was a God…'

Nobody passed any comment. Helene Weigel could be heard striking a match. She removed the glass cover from the oil lamp, lit the wick, and adjusted the flame. A few drops of water darkened the cloth on the low table. A storm was blowing itself out over the sea on the horizon. Brecht said, 'Thinking about problems that you can't solve is something you can well do without.'

Helene Weigel interrupted him and asked Maria, 'What did you do this afternoon?'

'I went to see the old fishermen's church. I had a swim.'

A cup clinked against a glass, Brecht drank schnapps, Ruth Berlau plunged her right hand into her dark head of hair. Brecht said, 'Talking about matters that can find no answer is something you can well do without.'

It sometimes happened that Brecht would summon Maria into his small study-bedroom. In general, this is how it went: Maria would lie down, and be slowly undressed. After the erotic phase, the master would take a shower. Maria surreptitiously photographed the documents on the wooden table.

Sometimes, she would also rummage though the waste paper basket and unfold the drafts of poems.

That summer, she handed over to a young female post-office employee four rolls of negatives that were sent off to Berlin. They contained the information that Brecht had sent three letters to Erich Honecker, a member of parliament at the time, asking him to intervene in favour of the famous actor Ernst Busch, whose name, in a song for children, had displeased the authorities. There were also letters to the musician Paul Dessau; he too, after the scores he had written for *The Trial of Lucullus*, was considered to be an eccentric formalist. Also a letter to Kurt Barthel, the powerful secretary of the Writers' Union, asking him, too, to intervene in favour of Ernst Busch, and letters to foreign publishers. Hans Trow, who spent his summer reading newspapers from the West, received Maria's parcels. He had the negatives developed, and concluded, 'There's only boring stuff in the things she sends in, we already know all that...' He leant back in his armchair and said to Theo Pilla, 'What I'd like to know is when she's going to get pregnant by the "master".'

Throughout her stay at Ahrenshoop, Maria left them more and more often, without a word. Her absences irritated Brecht. When he went into the bathroom, his little Antigone had hung a blue towel on the hook near the window and knotted her white, narrow bathing-costume to the window catch. The rag of puckered fabric swung in the draught, as if to taunt the ageing Brecht. Yes, this crumpled white swimming costume (and the little lace edging of the bustier) swayed and twisted in the morning breeze. This scrap of fabric taunted the master. He stopped in the middle of shaving, placed his shaving brush on the washbasin and fingered the delicate seam marking the crotch, where the fabric adhered closely to the mount of Venus. He wondered why it was that, when they were making love, Maria would assume that face of a dead queen, sailing to the stars, her eyes closed, as if withdrawn into the depths of herself. She slipped away from him; that was, indeed, all she ever did; she slipped away from the working sessions of the Berliner Ensemble, she slipped away from the theory classes, she slipped away down the stairs of the theatre, slipped away after downing the last drops of beer, slipped away for a swim, morning, noon and night, venturing out into the deep currents.

He made a mental count of the times. 'I've possessed her just four times since we arrived, the last time on the lino.'

He finished shaving, got dressed and picked up his walking stick before heading out to the beach. At first he saw nothing but the sun-drenched garden, the tarmacked road, cracked all over and covered with sand drifts, then he turned off down the path marked with tyre prints. He was caught up in the swaying of the sparkling waves when he reached the summit of the dunes.

Where was she?

He could see nothing but the vast horizon and the wavelets licking the rounded immensity of the beach. He started to make his way down the slope of the dune, taking off his light sandals, and getting pricked by the thistles. The crystal-clear sky was streaked by just a few wisps of cirrus. And whiffs of the dry odour of sea-weed… With difficulty, Brecht crossed a strip of pebble stones and looked towards the rocks. He recognised the canvas bag and, on a white towel that was spread out, the school exercise book which Maria used for making notes during the rehearsals for *Antigone*.

He sat on the edge of the towel and contemplated the sea. Waves, the cries of children, gusts of wind. So many possibilities for a good shag that never work out, he thought.

A solitary gull crossed his blue field of vision and uttered a raucous cry. The wavelets were so slow in the sunlight that you wondered whether this immensity wasn't one single deep, green, immobile mass. It was at this point that Maria emerged from the water, frozen, trembling, covered with droplets of water. Brecht heard his own voice, with its fake warmth, telling her, 'Come here, I'll give you a rub-down…'

She sat down with her back to him while he seized the sand-covered towel and rubbed down the smooth surfaces of her back in the same way you might scrape a wall. She stiffened, huddled up a bit closer to him, and Brecht vigorously rubbed down the length of her arms as if with a pumice stone; then, when he tried to kiss the red patches that were starting to appear along her backbone, Maria pulled away. Brecht slipped his hand between her thighs.

'D'you want to come?'

'No, not now.'

She stretched out on the bath towel. She attentively considered the pink, irritated skin on her arms.

'I just don't know how to behave with you!' he said.

They sat there, lulled by the roar of the waves. Sometimes, when she looked round, Maria Eich could just make out between her eyelashes the swaying of clear lines, passing shadows, brief metallic flickers on the waves.

A tapestry of clouds was rising on the left, and the sea was turning dark purple, with cold, bare areas. Maria got up, slipped on a skirt, and disappeared, a phantom sparkling down a thistle path.

After a heavy sleep, Brecht got up and gazed at the beach. It was completely deserted, so deserted that it hurt and burnt with its intense dryness. When he came back to the villa, there were some dry clothes on a washing line and, as they bellied out in the wind, the shirts were filled with the invisible torsos of fairground figures.

The hum of a small plane filled one part of the sky for a moment, taking an eternity to fade away. An empty silence: the garden, the deck-chairs, the iron table in the garden all moved through a liquid of strange, illusory immobility. The snail's pace of the clouds cast a momentary shadow on the steps.

Brecht reflected that the earth must be dead, then, or else had spun away from him, for in this empty silence, in the grass shining on the lawn, all that remained was the pollen of his own end, the marvellous, glittering pollen of his death.

Jauntily, he made a cup of coffee for himself and drank it, sitting on the steps leading up to the villa and waiting for the others to return.

13

On certain evenings at Brecht's, Maria Eich was relegated to the far end of the table.

One evening, she left the guests and decided to rearrange the furniture in Brecht's room a little. She discovered an Estonian Bible under the bedside table and started to read it. Between the pages she found a dried mauve flower, and began to daydream about the person who had placed the flower there.

Night fell. She sat motionless, the Bible on her knees, numbly absorbed in her reverie. She didn't feel sad. Then she heard steps in the corridor, the door half-opened, and a hand turned on the light switch; Brecht was standing there, holding a glass of fizzing champagne.

'For you.'

She drank slowly, already knowing the routine that would ensue. He undressed her, turned her towards the wall, and took her. She thought, 'He doesn't take me, he subjects me to a body search'. She clung to the yellow curtain, then clenched her fists when Brecht replaced his failing virility with a hair brush.

In the morning, she took a beach bag, stuffed her swimming costume, bathrobe and bathing cap into it, slipped out of the room, and fled through the green garden gate.

A radiant morning. A white sky, and already the villas and the big boarding house which now sheltered the children of the Nation's top bureaucrats were bathed in the heat. The air was vibrant, like wavering memories. Everything was delightful and majestic. You could sense the din of the waves, the rocks and the seaweed. Over on the left of the beach, a peninsula kept storms at bay. There was also a yellow field; and behind her, the open windows of a former casino that had been turned into an elementary school... She went for a swim... Throughout her stay, she always swam in the same spot. A channel of darker water, with a black line much further down – the remains of a destroyer. She stretched her blouse out on a pylon. Nowhere did she feel so well, so radiant. Her life melded into the eternal movement of the waves. Everything turned burnished and yellow, glittering. The sea sparkled at noon, and at four o'clock turned mauve. Her legs grew warm. She felt sleek and beautiful, nonchalant, dazed. A sail far out at sea took her by surprise like a mirage. Maria took off her sunglasses, and sipped the cold tea from her thermos flask. She swam in harmony. She slipped into the water. The sky formed a bizarre emptiness, then countless little cumulo-nimbus clouds rose and evaporated; thousands of glittering lights melted away, the sound of the rising tide was forever changing; she could forget Brecht and his gang; their narrow, ramshackle ideological constructions would fall down...

After a brief quarrel with Brecht, she discovered a pine wood behind the old water tower. Meadows, a tidal reservoir, the incredible brightness that percolates through this land of mist. One evening, she stood quite perplexed at a branch line. There were rails buried in clinker, a rusty level crossing, grass growing on abandoned platforms. She felt incredibly drawn to this place. The theatre – the real theatre of the world – was right here.

In Berlin, Hans Trow was so taken aback by Maria's recent reports that he slipped them into a folder concerning the directives for the reorganisation of the Baltic ports. He stuffed the whole lot into a bag, adding a note for Schrameck on the accountancy department's security arrangements. Then his tall shape was seen heading to the far end of the corridor. He spent the end of the afternoon in a swimming pool that had once belonged to the Luftwaffe ministry. He returned in the evening, with a little sandwich of rye bread and sausages and padlocked himself away in his office to reread the account of the conversations that Maria had had with Brecht and 'his gang'. The most surprising passage concerned the setting up of a calendar of the holidays that the New State would need. According to Maria, Brecht had drawn up and planned with great precision a series of official holidays. There was the Festival of Victory and the Night of Presents (why give presents at night? It was at night that the Nazis had presented people with Long

Knives). And the Day of World Struggle, the Day of Youth and, finally, the Carnival.

The report concluded that the Carnival was to assume a great importance as a day of disguise and mockery, 'a day of sorrow for the most sacred things and a day of mockery for the highest-placed personages'. He underlined the words 'mockery for the highest-placed personages'.

He was dumbstruck. For a moment, he sat in silence, thinking, 'who's really pissing around – him or her?'

Hans reread the last notes several times over and reflected that his bag wasn't big enough to contain such utter bilge. He tore the notes up, not just once but twice, and scattered them into the bin telling himself that he had never suspected Brecht of having a mind twisted enough to imagine a holiday on which the highest-placed personages would be ridiculed... It simply proved that Brecht wasn't quite all there. He was perplexed, and decided to see Maria earlier than arranged; he phoned her contact, a young drama student from Dresden, Ursula Bruckmann. She was doing a stint of work experience in the linen room of the Berliner Ensemble, where she ironed the actors' costumes. He dialled a number and let it ring. When no one answered, he started to feel a bit alarmed. He tried to phone again that evening and the person who picked up the phone, a certain Eckmann, who also worked in the linen room, told him that Ursula Bruckmann had disappeared several days ago. He felt strangely tense, then increasingly oppressed; then, the succession of the hours, the fatigue, the boredom... He decided to go over to her room in the student residences.

He spoke with a muffled voice at reception and the security guard, with the flair that soldiers – even in civilian clothes – have for recognising authority, did up his tunic. He took him to the fourth-floor room. It was a small white cell, there was tea in a cup, covered with a thin layer of scum; also, a calendar with the days crossed off until Monday, and pencil marks over the reproduction of a Dürer drawing that depicted an angel's head. An attempt had been made to increase the number of curls. On the washbasin were traces of soap; there was an electric radiator from the West, and, in the cupboard, a blouse swinging gently on a coat-hanger. Finally, there was a radio, oddly placed under the slats of the iron bed, and a strange perfume hanging in the air.

'Did she leave a long time ago?'

'Last Tuesday.'

'And who did you inform?'

'The steward.'

'Did she seem worried?'

'Who?'

'Ursula Bruckmann.'

'Everyone's got worries.'

Hans examined the locks, and the wire netting over the window. Then he straightened up and said, 'Give me the room key'.

He stopped to make a quick telephone call from a pub overlooking the Weissensee, then he returned home, placed the room key in a little box of Dutch cigars and reflected that the way young women kept disappearing was quite extraordinary. Bruckmann was no doubt simply one of the first. He knew that Otto and Grotewohl would not be best pleased. The fatigue, the boredom, the succession of hours. He started to examine a batch of photographic enlargements which Ruth Berlau had sent.

He gazed meditatively at the shot of Helene Weigel sitting on the cart in *Mother Courage*, with her peasant shawl wrapped over her head. That was hardly the kind of play that would get bums on seats for very long...

14

January turned Berlin white. The old black Skoda used by the intelligence services was starting to vanish under the snowflakes. Theo Pilla had pulled his gloves back on and was observing through binoculars the two windows, quite high up, with their Doric columns. Through the bare branches of an elm tree, Brecht's room was clearly visible. No curtains, no drawn curtains; Brecht's comings and goings... for a moment, the master came into view, pale, with his cap pulled down firmly on his head and the smoke from his cigar. Perhaps he was staring into the darkness of the Berliner Allee and the little veranda... Eventually, the window swung open; Brecht was obviously throwing something down into the rotting leaves on the ground.

Theo Pilla, numbed by the cold and a stint of observation that had lasted three quarters of an hour, mechanically counted the number of little squares on the transom. Just as in a dream, the longer he gazed at the windows, the more they seemed to come closer and then recede. Theo leapt when the car door slammed and Hans Trow made his snow-covered presence felt next to him; he took off his gloves and his hat.

'Well?'

'You don't have a blanket do you? I'm cold as a brass monkey.'

'What's happening over there?'

Theo muttered, 'Screwing around'.

Hans rubbed his hands and took the binoculars.

'Is Maria there?'

'In the shower room... She's in no hurry...'

Hans adjusted the binoculars and brought the black outline of the room into focus.

'You love that bedroom,' said Theo, wiping away the condensation from the quarter-light.

'Yes, I love bedrooms,' said Hans.

'Me too, but you love Maria's bedroom in particular.'

'What?' asked Hans.

'You love that bedroom,' said Theo. 'It's Maria's bedroom, and you love Maria.'

'Yes.'

'You've always loved her.'

'Yes,' said Hans.

'Me too... Mmmmm, only joking,' added Theo.

'I wasn't!' said Hans as he followed Brecht's comings and goings.

A smile lit up Theo's face.

'Why don't you screw her?'

'No relations.'

'How do you mean?'

'No sexual relations with agents. Never. Never at work, Theo, never.'

'She has expressive lips,' murmured Theo.

'Mmmm.'

'Too much so.'

'Too much what?'

'Too expressive, everything about her is expressive.'

'An actress' lips; everything about actresses is expressive,' said Hans. 'They are all tirelessly expressive...'

He continued to follow Brecht from one window to the other.

Bertolt was chewing on his cigar and flicking very rapidly through the western newspapers.

'He reads *Time Life* and *France-Soir*!' remarked Hans.

'That's his right.'

Hans watched the silhouette closely and pouted, looking doubtful.

'Why don't you screw her?'

'Screwing isn't the solution.'

Hans Trow gently opened the door to empty the dashboard ash tray.

'Why don't you screw her? You're in love... Why isn't it "the solution"?'

'Pardon?'

'Screw her!'

Hans put the binoculars down on his knees and looked at Theo.

'I love that woman. The only thing I can do for her is to help her get to the West.'

'All the same, it must be an odd feeling for you to see her wandering around from one bedroom to another with old fatso!'

'What have they been doing?'

'She tidied out two cupboards and then he read the papers, filling the room with smoke. Then they must have done things in the bathroom, on the bed, under the bed, I didn't see.'

After a silence, Theo repeated, 'Why don't you screw her? Take her over to the West and screw her in the West.'

'I don't want to.'

'You can't.'

'No.'

'Shall I tell you something?'

'No,' said Hans. 'Shut the fuck up.'

There was a long silence. Hans was wondering why, ever since his adolescence, he had concealed any feelings of love – why he was so ashamed of them. He remembered going for a walk through the wild grass, one summer, by the Baltic, an afternoon of high tide. He was going to declare his love to Ingrid, who was taking her final-year school exams like him. There were endless clumps of wild grass, the high tide, Ingrid who had shed her clothes and then gone swimming without a moment's embarrassment, while he had kept his clothes on, panic-stricken at the idea of expressing his feelings, tentatively turning phrases round and round in his head, brimful of idiotic or indecent suggestions, continuing to sit on a low wall as he watched the girl he loved go for a swim, sick with desire for her, aware of his total inability to make a move. He felt paralysed as Ingrid wrapped herself in a towel, then leant up against him, shivering, her shoulders spattered with drops of water. He can still remember her plait swinging on the nape of her neck; it became such an alluring and fascinating object that he viewed it in isolation as a mental image.

Yes, the girl had jumped onto the wet sand, laughing, she had run off while a storm brewed behind the villas.

'You just can't make a move,' said Theo.

'True,' said Hans.

Hans pulled up the collar of his overcoat and felt the cold start to numb his feet.

'Look,' muttered Theo, 'there she is.'

Hans was filled with a vague anguish when he picked up the binoculars to follow the couple's movements. The light changed in the upper room, and turned pink, as if Brecht had switched off the big ceiling light and just kept on the low lighting.

Then Brecht held out his arm and tried gently to tug the bath-robe off, but Maria dryly removed Brecht's arm from her shoulder. Hans put down his binoculars, and felt cleansed of all anguish.

He reflected that he would like to be in another life with this woman. Then he sat down again and thought that he preferred to be in this life with her. It was clear that Maria didn't love Brecht.

Theo Pilla's podgy shape was suddenly surrounded by blue smoke. A red dot glowed and crackled. Hans said, 'You shouldn't smoke'.

Hans saw his own face in the reflection of the

window, and the streaks of snow formed a lunar landscape that broke up the black design.

Theo said, 'It's the same for everyone'.

He added, 'You know, Hans, I adore women, and when I tell myself I've got one who's just some poor silly bitch, I can screw her!... but when I'm in love, I think it's just like I was seeing the Blessed Virgin. Do you know what I'm getting at?'

'No.'

Hans did up the top buttons on his overcoat, slipped the binoculars into their case and told himself that his life was nothing but a series of incomprehensible actions; but he at least knew that he loved his country, that he loved his job, his mission, and that he loved Maria Eich; but none of this really gelled. Sometimes he even found it hard to speak.

'Would you like us to have a talk about it one day? A proper talk?' asked Theo.

'No,' said Hans. ''Night, Theo.'

He unhurriedly walked back up the path between the fir trees. Along the lake, the reflections shimmered and broke like glittering snakes.

15

In the spring, several incidents filled Maria with unease. First there was a quarrel in the rehearsal hall when one of the Berliner Ensemble secretaries came to show them the photos of the company meant for press distribution. Everyone chimed in with the opinion voiced by one actress, a student of Slavonic languages, who preferred Maria with her face framed by a triangular scarf, making her resemble a Young Pioneer. Although Maria took a disliking to this photo, which seemed to turn her into an unwilling recruit and also hid her admirable hair, she was obliged to give in when Brecht intervened and said, in his ironic voice, 'Someone who's not very cultivated often perceives beauty when the contrasts are brought out, when the blue water is even bluer, the yellow corn even yellower, the evening sky redder and actresses have hair as curly as poodles...'. Maria preferred the amateur photos of her that sat on her dressing-room table.

In the corridor, after the rehearsal, Maria returned to the attack as Brecht was coming down the stairs. He assured her, with a hint of irritation in his voice, 'Everything which prettifies things makes them banal – it's foreign to art which uses alienation effects: don't you forget it!'

'Fine!' replied Maria.

The word 'fine' became one of her familiar replies. And when the atmosphere was too heavy, when she felt that she lacked that 'proletarian common sense' that pervaded the corridors like a spirit flitting through the forest, she would take refuge in a café on the Henriettenplatz and telephone her daughter Lotte. She took a sudden dislike to the valiant Weigel. She walked past the shops and the street windows in her district looking at her reflection to confirm her beauty.

Finally, another misfortune: summoned to receive her food coupons, tickets and a special form that gave her favourable credit, she was taken aback, on coming out of the offices, to see famished-looking children. They were trying to light up western cigarettes. She wanted to confide her worries to Hans, who expressed a certain annoyance on the phone. He explained to her 'that the instruments of work were properly distributed throughout the city'.

He repeated, with a certain somewhat mechanical zeal, that she had a mission to fulfil. He finally asked her how the rehearsals were going, and how she rated the pedagogic remarks uttered by Brecht. Had he mentioned Mao's China? 'Yes, an ardent yes, a pure and hearty yes,' was Maria's reply: she couldn't have cared less, all she dreamed of was having a cup of coffee with Hans. She yearned to go back home, bury herself under the sheets and wake up with him.

But Hans' voice at the other end rudely startled Maria out of her petty-bourgeois reverie.

'But what's making you feel uneasy? What is it that's so shocking? What you've told me is perfectly piffling...'

'But it's no joke,' mumbled Maria.

'Why?...'

'I have this sense that I'm going to fail,' she said. 'I dreamt of playing Antigone directed by Brecht. I dreamt of Greece, where everything is consumed in the sun. I wanted gods, a sea that sways and sparkles and dazzles, and I find myself in a house of the dead. Among people who divide the world into petty-bourgeois bastards and the radiant working class.'

'Yes,' said Hans, 'a land where the sea sparkles... Greece...'

Then they came back to Brecht.

'What does he teach you during rehearsals?'

'His remarks are very discreet. Brecht sits in the auditorium, he never disturbs our work, he's not a know-all and he doesn't give the impression he even knows his own play. He always has the attitude of someone "who doesn't know". If an actor asks him, "Should I go over here... when I say that?", Brecht often replies, "I don't know", but he makes suggestions, moves around, gestures – he uses anything and everything. There are moments when he can be a real hoot. That's the Brecht I like!... He loves to surround himself with very young pupils and, when he takes a liking to a suggestion, he picks up on it and makes it his own. He's open, relaxed, he never forces things... He hates it when discussions turn all psychological: then he brings them to a grinding halt...'

Even while she was saying this, Maria had the vague feeling that she was creating an image of Brecht that was too benevolent. She would like to have demonstrated that he didn't bother her, either emotionally or physically, that she could judge him without denigrating him. What she feared above all was that Hans Trow might lose all esteem for her. She longed to be able to hold forth in such a way as to prove to him her love of socialist duty.

When, with unexpected cheerfulness, Hans Trow told her, 'One day I'll come and watch the rehearsals, if only to ruffle the feathers of Picasso's dove!', she asked herself whether she hadn't attained her objective: that of getting an emotional response out of him.

16

Theo Pilla was jubilant. Among the mountain of forms and reports classified 'confidential', there was a note from a certain Richard A. Nelson who had spent a long time in Hollywood. As soon as Brecht had arrived in Berlin, he had passed on a few items from the files held on him. They didn't contribute anything very new about the dramatist, described by the Americans as 'of Communist tendencies', other than the fact that the FBI hadn't obtained permission to tap the phone in Brecht's villa at Santa Monica. On the other hand, his mistress and collaborator, Ruth Berlau, the beautiful Swedish actress, had been the object of constant surveillance. She was tailed, her mail was opened, regular reports on her were composed. What gave Theo considerable amusement was the number of errors he could enjoy picking out in the FBI reports. American paranoia had gone so far that some people had imagined the contract signed by Brecht with Warner, a copy of which was kept at the University of Illinois, contained coded information hidden in the juridical terms employed. There was also a report in which the author expressed astonishment that Brecht should show such an interest for cameras, in 1944. He, Theo, knew why: Brecht spent his time photographing the belly of the pregnant Ruth Berlau...

At noon, Hans Trow went off to get a saveloy sandwich along the Havel, then he visited a little museum devoted to inland water shipping. It had been preserved more or less intact since his youth, when he had visited it with his father. In the glass cases there were scale models, barges, yachts, knives, needles for sewing sails, and the faded photos of old rigging. Hans Trow wondered if Brecht really thought that the theatre would allow revolutionary forces to emerge. Was he preparing to flee to China or, as Maria claimed, to Austria? He had reread Maria's notes and opened Brecht's mail. Why had Brecht come to settle in this country where even the coffee is awful? When he was so fond of money, bank notes, comfort? And even his ideal type of woman inclined him more to Swedish or Viennese women – certainly not the women of East Berlin in their uniforms. Could Marxist materialism transform him – old anarchist that he was? What was he hoping for? What did he want? Fame? Revenge for the humiliation he had suffered in America? Was he harbouring some old petty-bourgeois family grudge? Was he dreaming of a new Athens? Was he chasing special privileges out of jealousy for the enviable status enjoyed by Thomas Mann?... What did he want?

Even his Marxism was an anachronism, with this cult of Rosa Luxemburg and Karl Liebknecht... You had to be an utter donkey to go after antiques like that. And then the delight he took, like some ham actor, in putting placards all over the stage, as if the spectators were all retarded.

He came out of the museum and crossed over a bridge. All that remained of an old patrician house was the flight of steps and a façade with blackened window ledges. Inside, a sea-swell of nettles swaying in the wind.

He returned to his office, tidied his index cards and told himself that in the evening he would go and watch the revival of *Mother Courage* that was re-placing *Antigone*. Then, he scrutinised at length the blackboard, picked up a piece of chalk and replaced the little number 2 by a huge 3. He wrote, 'Two world wars? No, the third has already started but no one pays it any attention...'

When he pulled on his mac, he told himself, that, who'd have thought it, he was going to be dealing with a dramatist whose medical files revealed that he had little chance of living beyond the next ten years, given the state of his cardiac muscle.

17

The relative failure of the performances of *Antigone* tarnished Maria Eich's image. Brecht swapped round the roles for *Urfaust* and gave her an insignificant part. He was starting to spend a lot of time with Käthe Rülicke.

This young actress was also involved in editing a literary supplement for *Neues Deutschland*, under Stephan Hermlin. She had a great deal of charm.

Two policemen attached to the new burgomaster of Berlin came looking for Brecht in the middle of a rehearsal.

They made the master climb into an old blue-black Mercedes: beech trees, birches, pines, maples, masons and building sites filed past the windscreen.

Then they entered a large building; Brecht climbed a flight of stairs, accompanied by a woman in a brown suit with her hair in a tight bun. He went into the burgomaster's office. Piles of tracts. On the oak panelling, a framed photo had been hung: Ulbricht in Moscow, with Stalin.

When he emerged from this interview, Brecht reported, 'The burgomaster didn't say hello or goodbye, he didn't speak to me once, and he let his two collaborators do all the talking. He merely uttered a sibylline phrase on my unpredictable plans that would spell ruin for the things that already exist. Of course, Ackerman and Jendretzky suggested some

Kammerspiele. There was also some talk of economy measures. They kept drumming this petty-bourgeois phrase into me: "To every man of the people, his official box at the theatre".'

He added, 'It's made me feel strangely dirty, almost demeaned. For the first time, I can smell the foetid breath of the provinces.'

Brecht was starting to get more and more irritable. He would take it out on anyone and everyone, with great unfairness that was quite uncharacteristic of him. He needed more and more bits of paper to guarantee him freedom of movement in Berlin, and he remarked on events with a terrible irony, which Maria Eich quickly jotted down in a notebook the minute his back was turned. His relations with the world, his attitude, his ways of relaxing, his success, his dinners, his questions, his future: everything was growing gloomier.

Even the housewives who did the cleaning for the Berliner Ensemble spoke in hushed tones. Then he fell mysteriously ill, and was unable to take part in the Writers' Congress. He sent a letter to its President. He set off for the town of Rostock, accompanied by Käthe Rülicke, Klaus Hebalek and Peter Patzlich. Here, they closely followed the last rehearsals for *Don Juan*, directed by Benno Besson. Käthe energetically took part in the discussions, made suggestions and took up theoretical positions that met with huge acclaim. Brecht had found in her not just a ravishing actress full of admiration for him, but an intelligent collaborator. A telephone call informed Maria of what was happening.

The resounding success of this adaptation of Molière's *Don Juan* meant that Maria entered a period of disgrace. She was now nothing more than a sex toy, lying on a shelf over the great master's bedside table. She was the plaything of a pimp. She kept saying to herself, 'pimp!', 'pimp!', 'an intellectual pimp, but a pimp all the same!', but she knew that the situation couldn't be boiled down to a mere insult. Words, even trivial words, were no protection from the immense disappointment that gnawed away at her day after day.

She would often leave her dressing room and wander down the banks of the Havel; she smoked cigarillos to boost her self-esteem. She had often imagined her life in Berlin in more glamorous terms. She realised the scope of the sly press campaign aimed at making Brecht out to be a formalist: she got involved in it, and sent in report after report. She endeavoured to give more and more precise information to Hans Trow. Her notes were now all unfavourable to Brecht. Maria who, only a few months ago, had still considered the Berliner Ensemble to be a gang of jolly guys and gals naïve enough to believe they could educate the people, now started to paint a black picture of them. She insisted on the conflicts, the boastfulness, the opportunism of those in Brecht's circle. She tasted the dark ecstasy of betraying secrets and sullying reputations. So they'd treated her as a puppet, had they? We'll see about that… Her notes, incisive and precise, reduced Brecht, his work and his conversations, to the level of the elucubrations of a petty-bourgeois pleasure-seeker who used dialectics to obtain privileges for himself. She described him standing at his desk, wondering how to court the wives of dignitaries, how to play fast and loose with the directives of the Writers' Union. She even handed over the drafts of a few poems in which Brecht confessed that he had dried up, and the only thing that now blew through his head was the wind of nothingness…

Hans Trow felt uneasy as he read these notes. He started to file them separately, and frequented the corridors of the Berliner Ensemble more regularly, on one pretext or another, just to check things out. He hung around in the offices of the administration, wandered up and down, listening. You could find him behind the high windows of the German Academy of Arts, in Kochplatz. Old actors opportunistically hauled out of moth-eaten cupboards complained of Brecht's methods. Reference was made to the agreements he had signed with a publisher in the West, and a climate of erotic banter that made the virtuous fighters for the liberation of the proletariat scent a whiff of scandal.

A young actress from Poland, in a seaman's jersey, with long shoulder-length hair, came one afternoon into Maria's dressing room and said to her, 'Were you his mistress?'

'I still am.'

'They say that he's had a lot of them – and still does.'

'Yes.'

'Have you been unfaithful to him?'

'No...'

Thereupon she declared, 'I can sleep with anyone I want to. Either way, who cares? Being groped by men, old or young, it's no big deal so long as they fancy me enough to fork out some cash. Basically, money *is* the only way of telling if a man fancies you enough...'

'I don't think you're right to say that.'

'We'll see – when you're in your coffin, being eaten by the worms; anyway, your dressing table here is your coffin. How many lovers have you had in your life? They really must have been queuing up for the privilege.'

She added, 'Do you have a child?'

'Yes.'

'Me too. And it pisses me off having to bring my little boy into a society that I view as senile, moronic and pretentious, with its stupid slogans.'

That very evening, instead of joining Brecht at the Seagull Club, Maria walked along the Spree. Barges, a line of lights from the other districts, the madness of living without a real nice hug from time to time. Burnt-out feelings.

She dreamed of going off to a Greek island where she could swim in the sea, of joining her mother and father who had turned into nice old folks warming themselves in the sun as they lay in their deck-chairs. She told herself that her footsteps no longer left any trace, that her shadow along the walls was shrinking, that her inner universe was being filled with wind and void. She longed for sparkling wavelets stretching out forever so that she could lose consciousness, turn into seaweed. She took shelter from a sudden shower. She listened to the rain in exactly the same way that she had used to listen to it in the wooded hills around Vienna. An old door that reminded her of the garden of her teenage years drew her towards it. Her cheek felt the coolness of the wood. An old rust-spotted radiator kept her company for a few moments. She wondered whether Brecht had a soul, a childhood; she could find no trace of either in him...

The West and the allied sectors were issuing threatening communiqués. There was a flurry of harsh, brutal propaganda. The West German newspapers raged against the Pankow regime. The Catholic Church, especially in Munich and Rome, poured oil on the flames. The snowstorms could no longer hide the incessant take-off and landing of military planes. Socialist morality was held up to scorn by leader-writers in the pay of the Americans. In the East Berlin ministries, teams of officials displayed an alarming zeal. There were long discussions about whether the Leninist theory of knowledge was being respected on the German stage. More and more people were being tailed, their mail was opened, their phones were tapped. Maria again felt she could be of some use in this vast movement of political revival and revolutionary enthusiasm. 'With a heart ever more pure and ardent', she dedicated herself to her duty, and displayed real expertise in bed with Brecht, giving herself, refusing herself, offering herself, feverishly noting down the least of his remarks.

Her intelligence work put her in a good mood, and made her feel curiously light-hearted: she experienced a bitter thrill at the idea of making her own contribution to the task of denunciation. Whenever she listened to the blackbirds singing near the kitchen, through the open window, she felt in harmony with them. They too were denouncing one another, from one branch to the next. The nature of the State, the nature of her work, and Nature itself at its most elemental were all driven by one and the same force. Honour... Pride... Virtue... the blackbirds... and her security file index cards were bringing joy to this new Nation. History, men and birds were ridding themselves of an old and rotten world as they sang. And they were singing the birth of a new order on the ruins of the old.

She felt herself to be a blackbird among blackbirds.

As for Brecht, he was sharing himself between three charming actresses. Delighted to find Maria in such a good mood, he was forever offering her small gifts. He would get up early in the morning, and sing as he boiled the kettle for tea. One morning, he announced that he was inviting her to spend the whole summer in his house at Buckov. Maria noted the information and then passed it on to Hans Trow with the dates. All of this ended up in the Ministry of State Security.

An orderly would come into a huge, light, spacious office, where General Orlow (his code name) would rise with an effort and take the reports with a grunt. A click of heels. He would dismiss the orderly with a sullen gesture and then, once the door was closed, started to slit open the envelope with his forefinger, pull out the pile of papers and scan them, pulling a face as he did so. The decadence of the West, *westliche Dekadenz*, imbued everything said by that fellow Brecht. He read quickly, then telephoned Otto Grotewohl, *Ministerpräsident*. He was holding the proof of the pernicious game played by Bertolt Brecht. Brecht? An enemy of the dictatorship of the proletariat. A separatist in a State that, more than ever, needed unity in the face of Yankee imperialist aggression. Basically, he would have preferred to have a conversation with General Clay rather than be obliged to read the reports on Brecht and his gang.

Buckov
1952

In February 1952, Brecht and Helene Weigel had been to see a nice plot of land on the edge of the Scharmtüzel Lake, one hour from Berlin. Old, tall trees, a modest, well-shaded little house. Higher up, a spacious house, white with a brown roof, and a large bay window on the corner. In addition, there was a cobbled patio and a greenhouse. Immediately, the property reminded them of their house in Skovsbostrand in Denmark, in 1933.

Brecht loved this house surrounded by pine trees, wild roses, the grey lake, the avenue, the old benches, a greenhouse.

Weigel settled into the huge house that dominated its surroundings, just as she had settled into the Berliner Ensemble. To receive guests, organise things, reflect, decide, write, and rule.

He chose the little house in brown bricks near the water.

Throughout the summer of '52, Weigel busies herself issuing invitations. She's perfect when it comes to organising the administrative aspects, changing the beds, preparing the menus, getting the furniture polished, giving directives to the cook. Maria Eich lives in the little house. She watches the master working when the morning is still fresh, when the lake is sparkling.

Brecht works early, in the freshness. Maria reads *Coriolanus* in front of the door, not far from the greenhouse, or leaning against the pine trees. Brecht has found an old table from a pub. Together, they repainted its iron feet, and two garden chairs. Brecht is spending longer on his siestas, when he reads a volume of Horace, but he finds him too indulgent towards second-rate poets – just as he, Brecht, feels that he is surrounded by councillors, dramatists and poets who are totally second-rate and compose cack-handed adaptations.

'They get into the rhythm of their poems like a cow plodding straight into a hole,' he says to Maria.

He reads the *Taglische Rundschau* and *Neues Deutschland* with great care to find out who's going to be attacked next. The Academy of Arts? Those in his circle? Himself?

Maria likes to take the oars of an old boat in the shed, fit them into the cleats, and go out rowing through the reeds. Often, she taps a barometer hanging in the corridor. Helene Weigel says to her, 'So, everything going okay?'

'Everything's fine.'

'It's warm...'

'Twenty-one in the corridor.'

'You look as if you're feeling the heat.'

'No, it's okay.'

'You *do* look hot...'

'Do you like it here?'

'...'

'You look a bit bored. Would you like me to change your bed for you?'

'It's been done.'

When he dozes off in his wicker chair, Brecht dreams more and more often of his parents. His father's toneless voice, his mother's voice close-up, his mother's deep concentration when she reads Luther to him.

When he sleeps, Maria picks up the master's glasses, and looks through the lenses, secretly nursing the idea that she will see with the eyes of genius. All she sees are the flagstones, the grass, the figure of Weigel standing in front of the greenhouse. She is smiling with an expression of modesty that is her pride. Maria puts the glasses down and leaves, reflecting that for 'emergency calls' she no longer has anyone, no contact. Is Hans still in Berlin? Brecht drowses heavily on, remote, wrapped in the toils of his cardiac fatigue. The streets of Augsburg appear, pale, the endless evenings, the swifts skimming over the tree tops, announcing the storm. The child Brecht asks,' What is there in heaven?'

'Paradise.'

'Are you sure?'

'Absolutely, Bertolt.'

'My brother Walter says the opposite.'

Later, when the glass panes of the greenhouse have turned dark in the sunlight and Brecht's back has gently slipped down the wicker chair:

'Are you coming home? Are you coming home, Bertolt?!'

'What about my brother Walter?'

'*He* wears a tie, he's clean, he washes his hands! He keeps his room tidy! He pays attention, his room isn't a pigsty!'

'No, I'm not coming home.'

When Brecht wakes up, the blue of the sky has turned black. The tremulous sky, the garden in the tireless beauty of summer, all alive and all-pervasive. He can't grasp anything, he feels a sudden terror, the little time he has left, the world is absent... A moment of meaninglessness, wobbling, unstable, fleeting. All he can see is Maria's swimming costume hanging on the fence. He longs for cool arms, a cool fresh body with the fragrance of the future. He swims in the dark water. Emptiness fills the lake to overflowing.

Shadow, rustlings, murmurs. The waters of the sky, the waters of the lake. The path and the tall trees. Maria and Bertolt head towards the same fence every evening. The gently sloping fields open out. Waves of grass, thick hedgerows, the tops of the black fir trees. The lake gleams. Clouds disperse with a slowness that suggests powerful winds high up. Brecht shades his eyes with his hand to peer up at this corner of the sky.

One evening, when Maria and he are out walking down the lakeside road, Maria notices a grey Mercedes. It's driving slowly along in the shadow of a hedge. It brings to mind a police patrol car. Maria can make out three heads inside, one of them that of Theo Pilla, but, despite her surprise, she continues to talk about the allocation of roles and the new rehearsals for *Coriolanus*. A single furtive glance at Brecht: anxiety. He pretends to be listening to her, she pretends to be speaking to him, then, all of a sudden, he interrupts, turns towards her and says, 'We've wasted our time!'

Later, he climbed the little wooden staircase that leads up to the attic storey; here he has set up a narrow desk on which he writes lapidary texts with a thick blue crayon. Through the tiny window with its thick panes, he looks out at the garden.

That evening, he wrote:

Standing at my desk
I look out of the window at the garden, and see the
*   elder bush.*
I recognize something red and something black;
and suddenly I remember the elder bush
of my childhood in Augsburg.
For several minutes, I ponder
quite seriously whether to go and fetch my glasses
from the table where they lie,
to see
once again the black berries on the red twigs.

2

Once the pleasant surprise of living in an attractive house surrounded by old trees has faded, Maria Eich starts to feel numb. She's in a curious state of mind. She feels more and more out of step. Her bedroom, on the north, is damp and looks out over branches covered with aphids. At night, she breathes musty air. Three days of quite strong wind have left big, grey, watery clouds low in the sky. The wind makes the leaves twist and turn.

Of course, she is still considered as the favourite; of course, she was noticed in Kleist's *The Broken Jug*; of course, she felt close to Ruth Berlau who, in her old pullovers, maintains her drive and freshness. Furthermore, Ruth has taken a remarkable photograph of her in the role of Eve, with a white bonnet and peasant skirt.

Often, early in the morning, between mist and sun, she slips out into the corridor, with her scarf on her head and some novels under her arm. She hides in the greenhouse, among the broken-down pots and the plants overrun by weeds. She takes a garden chair and sets it up against a thick, ground-glass cold frame that projects a watery light across the tiled floor.

From here, she can keep an eye on the guests who surround Brecht: actors from Dresden, female students, Paul Dessau… She stays here, daydreaming about the group of young women over there who are pressing Brecht with their questions.

With courtesy, and polite lassitude, he accepts the remarks and the questions. She herself has learnt from him this hard-as-nails friendliness that drains your heart but does, on the other hand, enable you to become an excellent figure of smiling feminine despair. In the many reports she composes for Hans Trow (twice a week), Maria Eich cannot stop adding to the notes about Brecht's past, as it emerges evening after boozy evening.

More than half her reports for Hans Trow concern anecdotes about Hollywood, on the American worker 'corrupted by a high standard of living'. In the process, she gets lost in bizarre details. She recounts three times over, via different witnesses, Brecht's time in front of the Committee on UnAmerican Activities, with the press, the radio, the cinema. She recounts how he gave a reading of his didactic play. She even finds cuttings from the American newspapers. She photographs them with the little bellows Kodak. She doesn't know that Hans and his secret service already possess a copy provided by another actress.

She draws up a long memo on how, the evening of President Roosevelt's re-election, Brecht was strolling through a friend's villa, a glass of beer in his hand, among the swirling dresses at a 'wild party'. Groucho Marx and Charlie Chaplin were the only ones to gather round a radio to learn the precise results of the elections. Maria also composes two paragraphs on Charlie Chaplin and the major influence he had on Brecht, especially in the case of the play *Mr Puntila and his Man Matti.* The idea that a boss becomes more humane when he's drunk, and starts to love his workers and accept their demands, but in the morning, when he's sober, relapses into being nasty – this idea was one he borrowed from Chaplin in *City Lights.*

Hans Trow wondered whether Maria's zeal for intelligence work did not conceal a secret fervour, with a hint of love, for Brecht. The 'I listen to all you say' of a source of intelligence is easily transformed into an 'I understand you'. The recent reports made such an interpretation possible – especially since, when Maria's reports were cross-checked with the notes of other informers, it emerged that Brecht must be working on 'top secret' texts that he communicated to no one in his circle, and wrote in the middle of the night. He lied to everyone, without restraint. He would spirit away certain poems, nobody knew how. Money kept leaking away to the Zurich banks...

Hans Trow had asked Maria to look into all this and to have a peep in the attic and behind the bath tub; she should arrange as many unexpected encounters as she could. But the question remained: Had Maria Eich entered the charmed circle of Brecht's admirers? By dint of the process of cross-checking his witnesses and then cross-checking them again, Hans Trow deduced that if Brecht's attempt at seduction had failed, his intellectual charisma, on the contrary, was working full blast, and Maria had fallen under its influence.

As for Theo Pilla, he refused to take Maria's reports seriously. But, one day, his attention was drawn to something in her report: one evening, Brecht, with an excellent French brandy in front of him, had made coarse fun of Anna Seghers and then, in a good-tempered jibe, had described Berlin – the whole city – as a 'witches' Sabbath where, to crown it all, there's even a shortage of broomsticks'. Theo left his office and placed the note under the nose of his superior.

'You'll like this, Hans... You hear? Berlin, a "witches' Sabbath!"...'

'One of our sources claims that Brecht has written several poems in code against Ulbricht and Grotewohl.'

'Do you believe it?'

'Of course.'

Hans spread out the contact prints on the marble table-top – 'photographs of photographs'. They showed a beaming Brecht during his stay in Finland with his mistress Ruth Berlau, who had never been as chirpy as just then. The snapshots show her in a birch forest, outside a tent, on the sea shore in a swimming costume, on the outskirts of an unknown village. She has a half-open blouse, a pair of light-coloured shorts, a sumptuous hair-do, a face bursting with happiness, a nice round behind: each of the photos is disturbing and alluring. An animal voluptuousness emanates from them. Such a fine summer, such an attractive young woman. Everything pointed to an erotic obsession.

Maria had even noted that, on the back of one of the snapshots, Brecht had penned in the words, 'My prick for your kingdom!'

The days flowed gently by in Buckov. Grey or bright, sunny or overcast. Brecht's complexion became paler, his jowls thicker, his tread heavier. Hans was bombarded with more or less useful notes. But the way Maria had changed was confirmed when she recopied a poem written by Brecht at six o'clock in the morning facing a leaden lake and a lowering sky. The poem, just the sort she liked, would indeed be a crucial item when one day this artist of the people was brought to trial.

O Germany, all torn apart
And not at peace within!
For in the cold and in the dark
Each side forgets its twin.

If you could trust yourself, you'd have
Such towns and meadows gay,
All would be full of joy and life,
All would be child's play.

The Stasi services here held a key piece of evidence. This poem, joined to Hans Trow's note, went right up to the first secretary of the Party who showed the 'secret' poem to Grotewohl. The latter simply viewed it as the satirical expression of an artist who had lived in exile for too long and was starting to turn bitter.

The note stayed in the files. They fully intended to use it one day. They just had to wait until the performances of the Berliner Ensemble had bored all the Berlin workers silly: then they could send the poem to Moscow.

3

Hans Trow and Theo Pilla were sitting in the shadow of the cowshed. They were keeping watching on lake. Over there, in the burning air, Brecht and the musician Paul Dessau were talking as they sat in front of a musical score placed on the garden table. Actors surrounded them.

Theo murmured, 'I can see him! I can see him!'

Sitting on a stump, Hans was laying a slice of salami on a piece of rye bread.

'I can see him! I can see him!!!'

And indeed, there sat Brecht, with his cigar, his cap pulled over his nose like a grandfather getting ready to take his afternoon nap.

'He's tired, isn't he?'

In his brightly-lit field of vision he could see insects skittering around, golden particles in the mass of foliage. He lost Brecht, then found him again; he was quite unable to master the focal length of this enormous pair of binoculars. A bright circle, illuminations, backlighting; devouring everything with the greatest attention; luminous shadows… finally he managed to stabilise the focus.

'He's no spring chicken.'

'Are they listening to him?'

'No.'

'I'd even say he looks wasted.'

'Really wasted?'

'Totally.'

'What are they doing?'

'Looking at him.'

'And what's he doing?'

'Talking; he's talking, and the others are listening...'

'Give me the binoculars.'

'It bugs me seeing all those guys who believe what he says.'

'He stuffs them full of blah-blah, theories... they find it reassuring.'

'Who?'

'The actors.'

'I wonder if they're really actors.'

'Meaning?...'

'Nobody's a complete actor.'

'He talks without waving his arms about – have you noticed?'

'He's holding a conversation direct with God. Deals with him as an equal...'

'He plays a very good game of poker.'

'This type of binoculars really hurts my eyes. I prefer navy binoculars.'

'D'you think they all venerate him?'

'Yes,' replied Hans. 'Pass me the binoculars.'

The insects were buzzing round the actors. Hans spotted a fabulous woman, the actress Käthe Reichel. Then in a circle of light he came across the ravishing face of Maria Eich, so bright... For a moment he caught sight of Brecht's unshaven cheeks – jowls, rather. He surveyed the faces of the young actors one after another. He felt a wave of nostalgia for a community of young people – when he'd been a law student in Leipzig, the discussions, the sense of intimacy, the friendly shoves.

Theo took the binoculars from him and started to adjust them for his own eyes. Then, after a long contemplative silence, he said, 'Sssssss…'

'What?'

'They're both leaving.'

'Let me see!'

'Hmmmm. They're both leaving… They're going off to hide…'

'Let me see.'

'It's true he's no spring chicken. He finds it difficult to walk…'

He followed Maria and Brecht as they melted away under the tall trees, following the stream. Their shapes were broken up by the foliage.

The couple stopped. Brecht was speaking; he stopped walking, waved his arms around. The bank of the stream was blasted by the sunlight.

Theo handed the binoculars to Hans.

'I can't see anything.'

'They're under the branches, look at their feet. I just love it!… The pig!…'

He added in a hasty murmur, 'I can only see their feet but I think things are working… yes, working extremely well!…'

'How do you mean?'

'They're feeling pretty spry.'

'What can you see?'

'Nothing, just Maria's red dress. She has a superb neck.'

The couple vanished beneath the oak trees.

'Okay,' said Theo, 'can I have those binoculars back, please?'

'Certainly not.'

4

She loved this grey weather, the lake's rather overcast shores, those red-brown rocks, those dull, bushy lines of greenery, that grass that swayed in waves beneath the breeze, those acid-green lichens. Clouds stagnated and billowed out so bright over the horizon that they gave you the feeling they were producing their own luminescence and spreading a gentle haze over the hills all around; the garden chairs, the canvas shoes drying on a window sill, the little wall and its wild roses, the odour of warm stone, the oak tree and its dark rustling, all diffused something that made your head spin. Deep in a corner of the sky...

Maria would tap the barometer in the corridor to watch the needle swing round.

One Monday, George Lukács came to visit Brecht. Maria saw them walking down the path to the lake, towards the reeds. Helene Weigel had dressed with elegance. She had a white blouse with a pointed collar, a flowered cardigan, an indigo blue dress with Persian designs, very nice canvas rope-soled shoes, and a little Swiss watch that Brecht had recently given her as a present. She went off to pick strawberries near the wooden pavilion where, a little later, Lukács took tea with Brecht. They talked about some obscure scribbler who translated Horace with as much sense of rhythm as 'a cow plodding straight into a hole', as Brecht put it. They talked about Faust, Goethe, and *Coriolanus*, and started to do some work on Shakespeare. Lukács pulled an old pub chair into the sun, on the grass. While he was talking, Brecht watched this massive man, his thick glasses, his shirt, his short sleeves, his rough fingers – and reflected that this man, the high priest of Marxist criticism, had been ceaselessly attacking him for twenty years. But Weigel had invited him... Brecht opened a notebook and jotted down a few ideas for his *Coriolanus*, thinking, 'This Lukács, fascinated by the problem of decadence, doesn't understand a thing. For him, class struggle is nothing more than an empty problem...'

Then, around midday, coils of smoke twist round each other on the garden table. Brecht talks of rose trees. Weigel brings the basket of strawberries and starts to wash them and take off the stalks. The smoke rises from Brecht's lone cigar on the edge of the table... The clouds, very high, are polite enough not to float over the middle of the lake.

From the barn, Theo Pilla keeps watch on the comings and goings of the little household. In the pavilion, Maria tries on Weigel's fur coats, bracelets, earrings, a fox-fur collar. She unfolds a handkerchief to sniff its perfume of lavender. Then she sets off for the forest and its resinous odours, takes off her clothes, slips into her swimming costume and dives into the green water. Her dive doesn't distract Brecht or Lukács. Lukács is sucking one of the arms of the sturdy pair of glasses he bought in Moscow. Brecht gazes at the ash-tray, fascinated. The slender wisp of smoke rising. Spirals, circles, sudden breaks. So many ashes. His first son who died on the Russian Front, Margarete Steffin who died in a Moscow hospital, all the dead actors, and those consumptives who still manage to hang on in the corridors of the Berliner Ensemble... Hitler has transformed his country into an ash-grey landscape. Pacifism is viewed with disapproval in both East and West. The ash-tray is still smoking. Brecht passes it to Maria, now back from her swim; she empties it into the bin, unaware that Brecht's head is filling with shovelfuls of ash.

In the afternoon, it gets even hotter. The lake glitters. The two security officers sweep the landscape with their binoculars.

Hans concentrates on Brecht's face, his jowls, the slight pout in the bottom lip. He looks like all those old men, rather bowed and dozy, forever sitting on a bench at the edge of the village, their eyes empty. Hans cannot help focusing on this heavy, bloated face, with its sparse hair; the short fringe, combed down onto the temples, suggests some shagged-out Roman emperor. He thinks, 'A mask'.

To judge from the little nods they exchange, there is a greater intimacy between Maria and Brecht than she is prepared to admit. In the double blue-hued circle of the binoculars, you imagine you can even hear how familiar and light-hearted they are with one another, while Brecht remains distant, tranquil, but not indifferent to the allure of the pretty Viennese woman. So far, she hasn't been very talkative.

Right now, everything is in suspended animation, the wind has dropped. Maria has gone back into the little house. In the toilet adjacent to Brecht's bedroom, among the grey jackets on the coat-hangers, she twists the little combination lock on a safe, then pulls out a heap of papers. She places the pages on the brick-faced opening of the narrow window, and takes photographs. Brecht's regular handwriting. Blue and rounded...

Behind the fir trees, young voices can be heard singing a Bach chorale, very far away, near the wood. Maria senses a presence, something like a shifting of the shadows. She flattens herself against the wall. When nothing happens, she carefully places the papers in the grey safe, scrambles the combination of the lock, presses the lever on the camera to wind on the film, and slips the camera back into its leather case. She hides the Kodak under the scarves that line the bottom of her canvas bag. When she re-emerges, the air is strangely muggy; Weigel, in a deck-chair, under the oaks, is doing a crossword with a red pencil. The flames of the candles flicker.

She asks, 'Would you like some tea?'

'No, thanks.'

Helene Weigel closes her eyes. Then she re-opens them and asks, 'Don't you think it's a beautiful night?'

'A really beautiful night.'

She adds, 'In a lovely spot'.

'Did you already know Buckov?'

'Not at all.'

'They call it the Switzerland of Brandenburg,' says Helene Weigel.

'Really?'

'Yes, the Switzerland of Brandenburg…'

There's a pause and then Helene Weigel says, 'Pardon?'

'I didn't say anything,' replies Maria Eich.

'I thought you said something.'

'No, I didn't say anything.'

'What do you think of Käthe Reichel?' asks Helene Weigel.

'She's charming.'

'Yes, I think so too.'

They hear the young voices rehearsing the Bach chorale as Paul Dessau conducts.

'What a wonderful place,' says Maria Eich, pulling her dress up over her knees.

'Yes,' says Helene Weigel.

'You're dozing off…'

'No, not at all.'

There's another long pause, the voices fall silent.

'What's Brecht doing?' asks Helene Weigel.

'He's reading Horace,' says Maria Eich.

'He's pretending.'

'No, he really is reading Horace.'

'What he actually reads are American detective stories.'

'American? I thought he preferred the English ones.'

'American.'

There was a silence.

'Do you think that Käthe Reichel will be good in *Urfaust*?'

'I imagine so...'

'Then she will be good...'

'Brecht has decided that she'll be good...' said Helene Weigel.

'So she will be.'

'But you personally,' asks Helene Weigel, 'do you think she's good?'

'No.'

'What a beautiful night,' says Helene Weigel.

5

Why, for several nights now, had Hans Trow kept having the same dream? He was travelling in a velvety blue restaurant car with white lamp globes. The menus were written in Russian, the train was speeding towards Moscow. He was drinking a cup of coffee when a Russian NCO, with a rather dodgy uniform jacket, sat brutishly down opposite him and gave him the news that his father had died.

'But my father's been dead for six years.'

'No, he died this morning.'

There was the regular rattle of the train, creating the impression that it was rolling over dead bodies. The NCO noted Hans' reaction and looked up at him, asking, 'Don't you feel anything at the death of your father?'

Then he left and Hans couldn't stop thinking that he was off to some dark festivity, that he was going to take part in an orgy of official slogans. Cities in the East were all thirsty for slogans. Everyone was concerned about moral life, everyone wanted to weave a new, bright-red fabric to hide the red of the swastika flags. They were in a hurry to get to a new orgy in Moscow. Hans told himself that the gods in Moscow were directing their wrath at Berlin. He wondered whether Berlin, like Troy, might not be destroyed a second time. Then he woke up and reflected that there was no doubt about it: leafing through *Antigone*, going over Maria's notes, and scrutinising Brecht's notebooks, all meant that he was imbued with the lamentations and angers of Greek tragedy. When he went off to sleep again, he was back in the train. He was heading into patches of mist on the steppe, then entering areas of darkness. Tunnels, ravaged terrain. Patches of snow. Forests of bare branches. Lonely pylons plonked down under a cotton-wool sky, single overhead lines. Bridges under repair: Moscow coming into sight...

While he was finishing his coffee, the Russian NCO returned, placed his cap on the table and said, 'We made a mistake, your father did indeed die six years ago. We're sorry about that.'

Hans could hear the clatter of SA boots tramping up to his father's office.

The curve in the track enabled him to see a big Soviet rail station. There was a crowd in uniform, singing; armfuls of flowers were presented by women in headscarves, and some delicious, very white bread was given to 'comrade' Hans Trow from Berlin.

Waking up, his mouth all furry, he remembered other women's choirs. He was eighteen and the peasant women from his village in Mecklenburg were watching him climb up a snowy hill, where he solemnly threw away a saxophone. He was discarding this symbol of his musical ineptness. The whole village was watching him, his mother and brother too.

They were filled with consternation.

He had brandished the sax and cried aloud as he

threw it onto the heap of snow-covered rubbish. The countryside had been glinting in the cold air. He would never be a great musician.

Why had Hans for some time now been haunted by the house he had been born in, his high bedroom, the cold air, the damp sheets, the dark bed in polished wood, the silence, the blaze crackling in the fireplace and the blistered wallpaper?

After midnight, feeling the grip of the damp sheets, as if he were imprisoned in a shroud, his mind too edgy to sleep, his senses on the alert, freezing cold, he would sometimes go and knock on the double door of his mother's bedroom. She was writing on a wooden table, with an old earthenware lamp in front of her. She never drew the heavy curtains shut, and points of light were twinkling in the distance; you couldn't tell where they came from. Hans' mother wrote, annotating bundles of paper and he, Hans, was now continuing the tradition, spending his whole life among bundles of papers, in the safe keeping of night, in the wakeful hours of insomnia, as a way of keeping the noisy banality of the passing days at bay and returning to the bright light of his conscience and his solitude.

He would like to have confided all this to Maria: his walks through the sandy fields, the landscape that was so flat, reduced to a few glittering lines, the unreal lightness of the patches of briar and the translucent willows and the very bright clouds which gave you the feeling of going nowhere but seemed to hide mysterious messages in their floating immobility. He would like to have confided all this to Maria.

Why, ever since he had known her, was he forever walking back down the secret slope to those poplar groves, as if he were attempting to renew hidden links? Why did he remember again the places of his childhood when he reopened Maria's file and her confidential notes that told him nothing he didn't know already?

The dilapidated serenity of the empty fields accompanied his walks across Berlin, at night, on his way home. The monotony of the Mecklenburg marshes, the spongy, darkening swathes of heather – it all came back to him, amazingly powerful and precise, and linked to Maria. Even the regular seepage of a trickle of water down a canal lock could, in its monotony, open a secret space that murmured something essential and hidden; why does he harbour within him the spindly shape of a few birch trees as if they were really the shape of Maria?

The hills of the sandy landscape, the canal as straight as a road, separating as it did the endless summers in two; the voices of his mother and his brother; it all came back to him, veiled but near.

6

Theo Pilla entered the Berlin office, took off his hat and mac, and placed on the desk a new note, and a brand-new pass, rubber-stamped in thick ink that still gleamed wet.

'There! The list of permitted newspapers has got longer.'

The note read, 'Bertolt Brecht is currently working in Buckov, Märk Bergland, Seestrasse 19, where he is allowed to receive the list of newspapers and reviews indicated below'. The previous list of German newspapers had been added to, and now included *Time*, *Newsweek*, *Life*, *Le Monde*.

Theo Pilla was also holding a brown envelope from the central office in Schumannstrasse, and from it he pulled out a series of reports from a source who went by the name of 'Isot'. Apart from a brief note raising, in terms of some asperity, the question of why Brecht should happen to possess the telephone number of Otto Katz, a Comintern agent suspected of being a 'Trotskyist traitor', there were two electrocardiogram reports dating from May, provided by Dr Müllereie of the Regierungskrankenhaus. Brecht had only a few months left to live. Then Theo brought out a three-page report on the draft of a will drawn up in English.

'Why in English?' asked Hans.

'Anglo-Saxon plutocracy,' joked Theo. 'Anyway, he's leaving it all to Helene Weigel. And look at the date.'

'18th May, the day after his electrocardiogram...'

Hans turned over the papers. His daughter Barbara would inherit the house at Buckov. His son Stefan would have the revenue from the plays performed in the United States.

'That'll buy him a nice meal!'

His collaborator Ruth Berlau was to receive fifty thousand Danish crowns on condition she bought a house that, on her death, would return to Helene Weigel...

When Theo came back with two coffees, Hans had read through to the end.

'Isn't there anything for Maria Eich?'

'No, nothing.'

'No mention of her name?'

'None.'

'Maria Eich doesn't get anything?' repeated Hans.

The rapid rattle of typewriters in the office next door was followed by stifled whispers.

Theo took off his jacket and undid the button on his shirt collar.

'And what does Brecht's electrocardiogram say?'

'General arteriosclerosis, sclerosis of the coronary and aortic valves...'

'Does he have any chance of pulling through?'

'So long as he doesn't move, or screw, or get angry.'

'It's strange...' remarked Theo.

'Yes?'

'...the way people of his age squander their

remaining energy trying to screw, to tyrannise others, to make up silly stories.'

'He does it in the name of art,' Hans pointed out. 'Don't you like art, Theo?'

'I'm not against it…'

'But you're not for it, either,' corrected Hans.

'Artists are people who don't want to grow up…'

'When I think she isn't being left anything…'

Hans picked up the draft of the will and then shut the file. He slipped it into Theo's briefcase.

'You carry it round in the usual travelling bag,' he said.

His hand started to tremble, the two men looked at one another and Theo asked, 'Have you seen her again?'

'No.'

'Do you think of her?'

'Yes.'

Theo picked up his leather briefcase and announced that the word was going round the corridors that Ulbricht was due, one of these days, to receive the medal given to veterans in the Spanish Civil War. Furthermore, one of Brecht's young collaborators, Martin Pohl by name, was so good at writing poems in Brecht's style that the man was being encouraged to keep on producing his pastiches and, simultaneously, being kept under surveillance. His talent might one day be used after the master's death. He'd been granted the privilege of going round Berlin with a typewriter bought in Hollywood. There were also rumours that the security services were going to be inspected at the beginning of September, and Moscow was sending more messages than usual.

Hans felt isolated, in an impenetrable fog; his life was turning into something unreal. The promises of a radiant future were growing more distant, while the past came ever more sharply into relief. He could again see his father and his disillusioned smile when the men came up the stairs, the clatter of boots, the brief cries, the panic-stricken servant girls and a father smiling at his son...

'Do you know him?'

'Who?'

'Martin Pohl.'

Hans started.

'Er... No...'

'It doesn't bother you, me talking to you?'

'No.'

'I see.'

'His photo's been going round the offices for quite a while and they're trying to find out what he was doing in Leipzig.'

'Who?'

'Pohl of course, Martin Pohl...'

'Ah.'

'Are you okay?'

'Yes,' said Hans.

'You're not a bit jumpy?'

'I am, actually.'

'You know what would do you good? You take the

car, a blanket, binoculars, and you go over to Buckov. Just a routine inspection to keep an eye on your protégée. You don't mind if I drink your coffee, do you?'

'No,' said Hans.

7

The black Mercedes makes its way slowly through a forest of outstretched arms, a sea of black uniforms, dark red armbands, then the Brown-shirts' parade. It was in Munich, before his exile, so far away... Brecht awoke. He heard the patter of the rain. He looked at his alarm clock. A grey light filled the air. The room bathes in this late afternoon light as it fragments into a dark, tangled tapestry; the shadows of the ash tree fall on his desk. The stapler, the waste paper basket and its wooden slats. How he loves letting the afternoon seep into his every movement, his plans, his hours. Examining Maria's skirt laid on the armchair, the braided belt and the little crest, the light grey of her blouse, the voices in the garden, the memories that resemble luminous postcards in saturated colours, with swimming, laughter, the bow windows of Santa Monica... the green, grainy shadows on the kitchen door...

He is drafting a letter to the people in charge of the Berlin border police. He is complaining about the way there are more and more checks at the control points between Berlin and Buckov, especially at Hoppegarten. There are endless hassles, checks on identity papers, the need to get special permission to transport the American typewriter, newspapers in the car boot, photographic dossiers on his collaborator Ruth Berlau. He complains in particular of the brutal tone so characteristic of the German police. He demands that they change their tone of voice when speaking to him, and stop those endless inspections of the car boot, of his papers – he has written that 'the passport is the noblest part of man'... He finishes his letter, 'Please understand me: I am not criticising the usefulness of these controls'. And he signs, 'with socialist greetings'.

Behind Ulbricht's braggings and his own there lies nothing but the one and only wretched German bureaucracy, a mixture of frenzied despair and mind-control, the same parades, the same trivialities, the brutality, the suspicion, the depravity; those boozing sessions in the tavern have stayed the same, from *Faust* to the beer halls of Munich: and today the same bullshitting into the microphones – the new modes of thought are exact copies of the old, with the audience, so petty-bourgeois, and incapable of understanding dialectics, the audience which clings to its classics. No revolutionary upheaval, no erotic flame...

The shadows shift tremulously on the ceiling. Other summers rise to the surface. For the first time Helene was wearing glasses with round lenses, and a metal frame that made her look like a professional seamstress; the children, still small, Barbara and Stefan climbing onto the garden table in Skovsbo-strand. The shadows of those summers stretch out across his inner winter. The touch of the cold tiles on the kitchen floor, the green and white rolling of the waves, ad infinitum. Stefan, a skinny lad, running through the garden in his swimming trunks; the rotting bench where he wrote, '*I have taken refuge under a Danish roof, a thatched roof, but, my friends, I still follow your struggle.*' But today those friends have disappeared. All that is left is the imperceptibly tiny snail-shell laid on a sheet of paper.

He is troubled by the odour of earth that wafts in through the open window. Earlier this afternoon, someone dug over the earth in the flowerbeds. He can hear the dry, inexpressive voice of Helene giving orders – Weigel, persuaded as she is that nothing fearful can happen in this Communist world of Berlin, since she possesses a Party card and the keys to the Berliner Ensemble. But over and above the repertoire, Brecht knows that there's nothing, neither an audience nor any support, nothing but Ulbricht's men spying, watching, reporting on and filing away your actions for Moscow...

While Brecht is closeted with Hans Eisler to work on the musical part of *Faust*, Maria Eich puts the lid back on a pot of white paint after re-painting the greenhouse door. She takes Helene Weigel's bike and rides three kilometres down a sandy road that extends along a wood of fir trees. The dry, resinous odour, hanging in the layers of warm air. The few drops of water on the fabric of her hat, the sound of the rear wheel catching, and then the exultant slow descent, the clouds on the horizon, the wind ruffling her hair and making her dress billow out, then the plunge into the forest, the clearing and the little black four-door saloon with its Berlin registration plate.

The car looks vaguely like an old Chevrolet. On the rear window, Maria recognises the dark red hardcover notebook that belongs to Hans Trow.

She gets off her bike, heads down a path and follows the furrow through the grass. She tries to guess where the two Stasi officers might have hidden. Then the idea crosses her mind that she has no great desire to come face to face with them. She gets back on her bike and continues down the path; she rides past the car feeling childishly tempted to slip a piece of paper under the windscreen wiper to tell them she's recognised them.

She cycles past luxuriant orchards. The dried leaves on the apple trees, the rustle of summer. Give up drama.

Become a teacher in a little town with empty churches, in one of those valleys where the dead generations rest and await new generations. She prefers peace and slumber to cynical calculation. She suddenly realises how widespread are the causes of grief. And then, she is overwhelmed by desire. She wants to see HIM and starts to rummage feverishly for his telephone number in her bag. Or else return to the car and scrawl a note and leave it under the windscreen wiper.

Then there was a gentle rustle in the grass, the white gleam of a short-sleeved shirt, and Hans Trow appeared. Maria examined his face closely, and was struck by his tan. She thought he looked tired, then the impression was effaced by a smile, as if he were emerging from a long, fresh night.

Hans and Maria stood there, hardly moving. Maria had left her bag half-open, and her bike leaning against her hip.

'I have the impression I'm being indiscreet,' said Hans.

'It's your job,' replied Maria.

'If you like…'

For the space of a moment, they experienced a magical sense of togetherness. Then Maria took the plunge.

'I'll come with you to your car,' she said.

'I'm not sure that's…'

'What?'

'Entirely necessary.'

'So much the better,' she said, jauntily.

They moved forward into the oblique yellow of the meadow that seemed scorched in the heat. Maria started to hobble. 'My sandal,' she said. She took off her light rope sandal and gave it to Hans, who examined it.

'There's a nail coming through inside.'

There was a moment of suspense between them; he rested the sandal on a stone and tapped it with one of those pieces of flint that you find on bad roads.

'There you go…'

'Is that it?' she asked.

Hans felt a curious sense of solitude, a small, shooting pain, when he saw the radiance of her face, floating there. She herself seemed to be floating, that was what stupefied him. He heard her voice saying, 'Aren't you bored silly?'

'Why? Because I'm keeping tabs on you?'

'Yes.'

'But I'm also protecting you.'

'What will you be doing in five years' time?' she asked.

'I'll be even more deeply immersed in the plodding labyrinthine labour of bureaucracy. What about you?'

'Me?'

'Yes, Brecht will be dead. You won't be able to marry him.'

'The idea would never have occurred to me.'

They were coming up to the car. Theo Pilla was already sitting in the back and nibbling a sandwich wrapped in a piece of greaseproof paper.

'What about you?' repeated Maria, 'what will you be doing?'

'You mean tomorrow? I'll read some report or other informing me that the visa section in Moscow is getting pernickety and jumpy, and how many secret agents have deserted, how many cars have gone over to the American sector, how many registration plates have been photographed outside the hotel in the British sector where General Schwerin, Adenauer's adviser on military questions, is staying.'

He added, 'I'll still be doing the same thing at fifty.'

'Why?'

He hesitated and reflected that there was nowhere they could meet now or tomorrow, by chance in some reception, nor even in one of those swimming pools in the outer suburbs towards Potsdam. Theo Pilla was evidently leaning forward trying to listen through the lowered window to what was being said.

'Why couldn't we see each other, you could simply come to the rehearsals, one morning?'

'Yes, I could, but I won't.'

Hans opened the offside door.

'I've lived with one woman, then with two. It'd be a mistake.'

She came up to the window and, strangely, he closed the door.

'Are you going back?'

'Yes.'

There was the persistent echo of the car purring away through the trees and bumping along the path, and the feeling of abandonment, the powerful and painful music of a scorching hot summer's afternoon and, over there, explosions of water: swimmers, probably. Why was everything so painful, why this exile, this solitude, this emptiness? Maria wondered what awakening would one day ring out. But she continued to push her bike along; everything was white with heat as she approached the lake. She could hear the voices of the swimmers and the tap-tap of a ball.

She headed straight into the house, slipped on her swimming costume and went for a swim. As she swam towards the willows, she gazed at the fir trees, the terraced hills, the greenish and brown rooftops, all that pastoral sweetness that, as evening fell, filled her with peace.

After dinner, Brecht left the table and his guests.

He draped his jacket over his shoulders and walked over to the lake. The avenues were full of insects; some of the foliage cast stripy shadows.

The nocturnal solitude was full of a mysterious glimmer.

The lake conveyed a kind of farewell. The confusion of everything, the blessed anonymity of everything flooded into him and filled him with a gentle and quite new sadness.

Everything melted together, the music of the inner world and the outer, merging together, transitory.

Brecht was an island, an island surrounded by pastures, reeds, tall trees – the essence of a dream to which he had never bothered to pay attention. His consciousness was inundated by a universe whose opacity he himself had tried to clarify. He hadn't given up his earthly dream, but the waves of his own death rose on every side, drowning him. He sensed the grey planet rolling hopelessly towards a world that would no longer be his. A world which would no longer talk about him. He swiftly turned round. The lamps in the house were lit and he could see someone (was it Helli or Maria?) washing the dishes in a bowl.

8

Maria takes two sheets of paper: Brecht's blue handwriting, jottings for his diary, in which he describes Ulbricht and his gang as 'unpredictable', 'superficial' and 'vain'. Five clicks of the camera shutter. She rewinds it, and slips back to her room. She pops the camera into her canvas bag, licking the flap of the Kodak film and sealing it with the sticky paper.

Later on, she goes out for a breath of air. The steps in front of the house, with their two decorative cement balls. The long wooden table, the empty deckchairs with their canvas that sometimes preserves the imprint of the sitters' bodies. That light, the colour of mint cordial, those empty glasses that suggest a phantom cocktail party. The guests: Käthe Reichel, Egon Monk, Hans Eisler. Helene Weigel is folding the Berlin newspapers under the green roof and the little iron columns of an old-style pavilion. She notices Maria sitting on the landing and caressing the surface of the water with her feet. 'She's bored,' she thinks; so she gets up and waves to her.

'Maria? Maria…'

Maria turns. She's looking very young in the morning light with her black dress and its flower pattern. Maria comes up the steps, reaches the pavilion and pulls up a wicker chair.

'Well?' asks Weigel.

There was a short, uneasy silence that quivered between the two women.

'You look really great,' said Helene.

'Yes,' said Helene stupidly, feeling awkward and embarrassed.

'Do you fancy some champagne?'

'Yes…'

Helene pulled the bottle of champagne out of the watering can filled with cool water. The two glasses fizzed and bubbled.

'Brecht really likes your youthfulness.'

'Yes,' said Maria, 'he really likes young people in general.'

Maria was reflecting that she ought to say what a nice sunny day it was, and not too hot.

She said, 'What a nice sunny day it is, and not too hot.'

'Really, you have a sumptuous little body,' said Helene.

Maria smiled without quite knowing why.

Helene continued, 'Brecht told me I had a sumptuous body'.

She added, 'In 1929'.

There was another silence.

Helene said, 'Brecht told me, "You have such a sumptuous body they ought to put it in an anatomy lecture hall". Didn't Brecht tell you that?'

'No… No… I don't think so…'

'I'm his corpse. His bad conscience is always a corpse. Look at my cheekbones, my forehead: I'm his skeletal ghost. But when I was young, I was very beautiful.'

The sun shone, then darkened, disappearing behind a cloud.

'Congratulate me,' said Helene.

'What for?'

'For living with him for so long.'

'Congratulations,' said Maria.

'It's not 1929 any more,' said Helene, 'I'm going to leave him.'

'No,' said Maria. 'Divorce?'

'Yes. Divorce.'

Later on in the evening, surrounded by the good-humoured guests, Helene Weigel said, 'What about you, Maria, don't you know any jokes?'

'No.'

'Everyone knows at least one. Don't they tell jokes in Vienna? No Jewish jokes?'

To show willing, Maria repeated a Jewish joke that a stagehand at the Deutsches Theater had told her, but she got muddled.

'That's a strange story of yours,' said Helene. 'It isn't by any chance anti-Semitic?'

'But...'

'It's an anti-Semitic joke, isn't it?'

'You're trying to slander me in the eyes of the people round this table...'

'People? Our guests!' exclaimed Helene Weigel. 'People? You think we are just "people"?... What would you be without us? A provincial actress...'

Maria hesitated, then put down her napkin and left

the table. There was a sound of the glass door slamming. Brecht said, 'Cigar?'

He added, 'She's not anti-Semitic... Helli!... stop it...'

'Her father was anti-Semitic, she has an anti-Semitic husband... I can wind her up a bit if I want to, can't I?'

The night had plunged the middle of the lake into darkness. Some lamps and a few candles had been brought out. Curious night lights had been set up for a village party on the other shore of the lake.

A slim yacht, with a dark blue hull, glided by beyond the oak trees. Tiny reflections glittered along its hull, like the flakes of some rare metal.

9

Brecht's letter complaining about the endless inspections at the Hoppegarten control point, on the
Berlin-Buckov road, was lying on Hans Trow's desk.
Theo himself was trying to decipher the notes written
in the margin of Brecht's *Coriolanus*, a document
that would be heading, in its grey folder, for the
archives on the top floor of the brand new Stasi offices.

Hans held out the latter to Theo Pilla who turned
on his heels and went over to the window where he
could more easily decipher Brecht's handwriting.

With his knee leaning against the radiator that gave
out hardly any warmth, Theo looked over the two
sheets of paper. On the other side of the window,
distant chimneys were nonchalantly emitting a plume
of smoke into the pale light of the morning.

'I'm extremely sorry to hear this,' commented
Theo.

'Me too.'

'Still, it's less serious than if his typewriter was
broken.'

'It never breaks.'

'Oh yes,' said Theo, 'it's true that our military tone
is a bit of a bore…'

'Yes, we've quite lost the tone of good old Prussian
politeness.'

'Sometimes, we miss it.'

'Yes, we all miss it.'

'Yes, this "State Security" tone gets us into trouble at times...'

'No, it gets *him* into trouble...'

'There are certain young soldiers who aren't actually all that smart.'

'We're not in the Prussia of Frederick II any more.'

'Even in the Prussia of Frederick II, there were certain military chappies who weren't actually all that smart on the politeness front...'

'That so?'

'Anyway, letters like that – there are cartloads of them on the top floor... and in the archives.'

'How much energy old Brecht squanders! He could have written a nice scene in a play instead of wasting his time writing this letter...'

'I can't believe my eyes. To think that he wasted so much ink, so much time, so much effort...'

'If you take a closer look, there isn't much sign of any particular literary gifts in this letter...'

'You even start to wonder if it was really him who wrote it.'

'What shall we do with the letter?'

'We'll file it away.'

Hans looked up and gazed at the factory chimneys in the distance; the sky, now greyer, seemed strangely restless.

In four months' time, it'll be snowing. Soon, coal in the stove, steaming mugs of tea, files being moved from one floor to another, the secret conferences on the top floor, the gloomy barges and their cargoes of coal, the repeated squabbles between the Academy of Arts and the Berliner Ensemble, the virtuous Nation, the hypocrisy of artists, the day-to-day routine…

10

Theo Pilla had resumed his surveillance. He'd been sent a new and more powerful pair of binoculars from Moscow. So he could see Brecht sitting on a bench, leaning against the little stone wall, the details in the woodwork of the shutters, Maria passing in a haze of light, wearing a red and black dress that she wore Spanish style, the table cloths and sheets hung out to dry, Brecht's pen covering the paper with blue ink. 'The next time Moscow sends me a pair of binoculars,' he said to himself, 'I'll be able to read straight through the paper, if the pages are held the right way round.'

More than ever, Brecht could sniff the inquisitorial atmosphere and sense the edginess of the circles around Ulbricht. The newspapers kept saying that Adenauer was not only inciting the American troops to dig in for a long stay in Germany, but was demanding that nuclear weapons be deployed on the territory. Hans Trow's staff already possessed, in brown paper covers, photographs – admittedly rather blurry – of 280 mm automatic guns, stockpiled in Arizona.

In the western newspapers, the headlines announced that the head of the East German government, Walter Ulbricht, had considerably reinforced the Ministerium für Staatssicherheit (the Stasi, for short), and was recruiting new informers every week. Every apartment building, every block of flats, every building site, every barracks, every cultural commission, every new district was to have its own informers. The organisation's far-reaching tentacles were reaching out menacingly for everyone. Hans told himself that he lived in a world which preached peace, but sensed that at any moment the sun could disappear from the city's rooftops, hidden by the grey mist rolling forward in a huge wave; he knew how the heat could radiate from the walls, penetrate your clothes and glue them to your skin. The dark and dazzling image of the nuclear conflagration often floated through Hans' mind. To see the sun no more, to know that Maria's face could be reduced to a young woman's smile imprinted on plaster. All of this haunted him. Just as he was also preoccupied by the fact that covered trucks were bringing groups of men, civilians, to the building entrance. Workers were taken down into the basement where they remained sitting on benches, under the wan light of electric bulbs. In the corridor, an Alsatian dog trotted by, yapping, obedient to the commands of a Russian soldier.

Hans knew that the phones were being tapped. The mail was opened, the neighbours on the floor were interrogated to find out who exactly was working for 'warmongering imperialism'. The Moscow trials worried Brecht, but they also worried Hans Trow, who every day, in his mail from Moscow, received instructions and discovered new possible counts of indictment: *cosmopolitanism, Zionism, deviationism.*

A note on grey paper, classified 'top secret', asked Hans Trow to put Helene Weigel under surveillance because of her Jewish origins. Hans Trow was overcome by a rush of anguish, pushed away his cup of coffee and went to the toilets where he crumpled up the note and pulled the chain. He wondered whether the services he worked for wouldn't end up condemning every last little earthly joy, and he forced himself, painfully, to question his own activities. As he gazed through the little window, he noticed that new stretches of barbed wire were being unrolled round the military camp and its petrol reserves; how many times would they destroy Berlin? How many times *could* you destroy an already destroyed city? His conscience told him: times aplenty. The dust, the petrol, the ashes, the wind: it can all explode, collapse and start all over again. Then he buttoned up his uniform. The courage of a decent man remains his secret. He would safeguard Maria's existence, even if he had to leave his own post. He would procure false papers for her, he would save at least one person, so that she could save her life and take her daughter Lotte with her. It was, after all, more than just a paradox that her Nazi husband, a dodgy music-hall artist, a handsome hunk of a guy in a polo neck sweater and sunglasses, should be in Portugal, sipping a glass of sweet wine on a sunny beach. It was the Nazi bastards who were alive, while the living, over here, were filled with fear.

Stalin's diplomatic notes recommending German reunification were, so they said, thrown in the bin by Secretary of State Dulles, who positively fell about laughing at the idea. Any idea of 'collective security', a Soviet concept, was rejected.

In Berlin, much was made of the workers' movements and the discontent prevalent on the great building sites of reconstruction. The atmosphere in certain districts deteriorated, and security agents summarised the situation as one of a probable imminent uprising; the effect was to make Ulbricht's positions even more intransigent. Hans Trow was asked to keep a particularly close eye on the dissident tendencies of 'that gang of pacifists' around Brecht who for his part, with his own idiosyncratic brand of anachronism, was – according to Maria Eich's reports – tempted to leave for Mao's China. Brecht would stand for ages transfixed by a map of China pinned up in the corridor that led to the bathroom.

More and more reports came in on the subject of regrettable formalist tendencies... The reinforcement of political surveillance over the artistic milieu was taken very hard. At the beginning of August, when Brecht learnt that, by decision of the commission, the Academy of Arts had by full official decree excluded Ernst Busch, the great actor and singer, from his own publishing house, he was extremely shocked.

Through his binoculars, Theo Pilla could make out Ernst Busch standing in the sunlight, wearing a grey short-sleeved shirt and black trousers, taking off and putting on his glasses as he listened to Brecht and Helene Weigel, who were sitting on the bench that leant against the old rose bushes. So, rightist deviationists were being invited to Buckov.

In addition, in her reports, Maria made a point of insisting on Brecht's 'right-wing' reading matter; he lingered every morning over *Newsweek*, *Quick*, *Münchener Illustrierte*.

One evening, Maria noticed that Brecht had locked one of the drawers in his office. Against the advice of Hans Trow who had told her, 'Never use the telephone when it's a matter of some delicacy,' she telephoned from the village of Buckov. She said she needed to see Hans Trow. But Theo nonchalantly replied that she simply needed to find the key ('it must be somewhere'), the drawer in question must contain a few bank statements and some 'rather smutty letters', maybe a deviationist poem, filled with bitterness, penned by that 'bloke who could have it off with all the prettiest girls in the regime'. His tone hardened as he pointed out that, in the meantime, he wanted to know what Ernst Busch was saying to Brecht and Weigel, 'to the nearest comma'. Finally, he muttered that it would be a good idea from now on if Maria could avoid systematically telephoning for the least 'piffling little thing'.

Maria had the crazy idea of returning to Berlin. She had to see Hans Trow. He would never have replied with such casualness and contempt. He was the only one who could gather, analyse, select, clarify, put in perspective, believe in virtue and the joys of Duty. She'd had it up to here living in this thuggish atmosphere, surrounded by intellectuals who were old bores, and tyros who were hypocrites, whose only thought was to win favours and get jobs. Hans Trow, on the other hand, had turned to her because he had sensed in her an 'ardent heart' and, in this cynical milieu, he was the only one who seemed to look after his informers.

During the dinner, Brecht had a row with Maria because she'd taken his razor blades to shave her legs.

'Please, Maria, do *not* touch my razor blades! I don't want to have to tell you again.'

Around the garden table, the chattering fell silent. The only sound was the buzzing of a wasp drowning in the carafe of water and the murmur of the lime trees.

Helene Weigel tried to get the conversation going again. Candles were lit. Maria felt strange, she reflected that she had fallen into a trap in the same way that the wasp had fallen into the carafe. She heard Weigel, Brecht and Ernst Busch laughing. They were reading a brochure, sitting on the steps leading up to the house. She decided to get a knife from the kitchen and force open the locked drawer. She must execute her mission with sang-froid.

The rest of the evening dragged on. They were sitting in silence round the table, watching Brecht play chess, while the time fluttered by like the midges. Maria felt that she had been definitively disgraced when Helene asked her why she didn't have her Party card. But who, here, was rejecting whom? Perhaps it was Maria who was sending this band of sly schemers packing. They were all apparently pretending to take a great interest in how Brecht would move his knight…

Suddenly, the weather turned stormy and chill. Maria quickly and quietly headed off through the patio to that little door that led directly to the office which was illuminated by a night light surrounded by a shade of cracked brown paper. She tried to force open the drawer and realised that she only needed to lift it up, slipping her hand underneath it, for the bolt in the lock to slide out.

She discovered the drafts of Brecht's letters complaining to Ulbricht about the opinions expressed at official meetings about his way of adapting the classics. Then there were lists and random remarks under the felt fabric at the bottom of the drawer.

Maria unsealed a brown paper envelope. It contained FBI reports, in particular one dated 6th June 1944 (an unforgettable date). The agent Thompson reported an interview with the Czech consul in Los Angeles, Edvard Bene. It was thought that Brecht was inquiring about the possibility of obtaining passports for himself and his family, with a view to returning quickly to Europe.

On 16th June, another FBI note mentioned a meeting Brecht had with the Russian Vice-Consul,

Gregori Khcifetz. In a thick white envelope sliced open on one side by a simple scissor cut, there was a letter from Ruth Berlau dated 26th July and posted at Pacific Palissade. The beautiful Swedish girl, now pregnant, had taken the plane from New York to California, where Brecht could attend the birth. In it, she informed the father-to-be that she was staying near the home of the actor Peter Lorre (who had played the main part in the film *M.*), in the Motor Hotel chalet. The tone of the letter was tense. Two FBI reports by the same Thompson verified with complete certainty that the 'little dark-haired man with a cap and a grey cotton jacket' who had come to this 'Motor Hotel chalet' was indeed the Marxist dramatist Bertolt Brecht. Finally, one last FBI report noted that, on 3rd September 1944, a certain Michel had been born to the Swedish actress Ruth Berlau in the Cedars of Lebanon clinic. A pencilled note had been scrawled in the margin, saying that the baby had died a few days later.

Maria slipped the documents into her bath towel and put the felt cover back in place on the bottom of the drawer. She could take as much time as she needed to photo the documents. She was touched by what she had just found out.

Of all the notes, letters, extracts from work diaries, and poems that had passed through her hands, it was this report on the birth of the son of Brecht and Ruth Berlau that really overwhelmed her. She thought, 'Never to have another child... never... that is the real curse'. Leaving East Germany, alone, would indeed represent a failure for her. A political failure and a failure in her private life. She could see herself traipsing from one boarding house to another in the American sector with her daughter Lotte, the solitary meals, the countless couples all around her, like an inaccessible happiness. She imagined the gloomy evenings spent at table, the few words exchanged between a little girl who was an only child and a woman who was wilting away, far from the theatres, from men, from Hans Trow. She wouldn't even be able to see her childhood friends, since Vienna was under Soviet control.

She was turning all this over in her mind when she heard a small group chatting in low tones, not far from the open window, with laughter and the sound of glasses clinking. Maria moved back, away from the patch of sunlight warming the parquet floor. She had never imagined having to wander round with her little girl. One day, Hans Trow would end up in a ditch, liquidated by his colleagues in Moscow... Yes, solitude would encircle her, the circles would extend beyond Mecklenburg, beyond West Germany, and touch the Baltic shores.

Suddenly, one day, with the landscape of a flat, grey, cold and monotonous sea, something else would begin. What? Another life.

It was then that Maria heard Brecht's voice in the corridor.

'Maria!!! Maria!!! Come with us!...'

Maria closed the drawer. She flattened herself against the wall.

Brecht came in, his face blood-red and his forehead beaded with sweat; he was sucking on a Corona, and smiling.

'You always come into my bedroom when I'm not here; and when I come in, you go out...'

Maria didn't try to smile. Brecht continued, 'You go off for a walk when it's raining, but when the sun's shining you shut yourself away in your room. When I feel aroused, you button up your blouse and press your thighs together, and when I drink champagne, in the morning, with my guests, you come sniffing around in my bed sheets, looking to see if I've hidden away a few pathetic ideas, if I've stuffed a Swiss passport under the mattress, if I've made a note saying I'm planning to assassinate Comrade Ulbricht. I don't know if you'll eventually find what you're looking for, Maria, but you're a bloody pain in the arse. I just wonder what I'm going to do with you.'

He corrected himself, 'With you, my dear...'

He cleared his throat and lowered his voice.

'There's some of the blueberry tart made by Helli left. Would you like some?'

Through the window came two butterflies, fluttering round one another, noises from the garden, birdsong, fresh air, shifting shadows.

Brecht took from his shirt pocket a propelling pencil, and found his notebook in the pocket of his linen jacket hanging on the back of the door. He jotted something down. Maria stood there, open-mouthed, gazing at Brecht's bed where it sagged in the middle, and wondering why she herself couldn't stand the idea of slipping between Brecht and the wall. She needed air, she always needed air. She felt like going for a long walk through the peace of the forest, through a holy forest, with, at the end of a path, the black car and Hans Trow, waiting.

Brecht retracted the lead in his pencil and looked at Maria.

'Let's make it up, today.'

He caught her by the shoulders, pulled her towards him, and then sucked her ear lobe.

'Come on!'

He whispered in her ear, 'And just be smiling and friendly, be nice to our guests'.

11

Hans was spitting into the water. He was like a schoolboy, in the middle of his holidays, in Berlin. He gazed at the closed doors of the Deutsches Theater. As it was starting to get hot, he took off his jacket and went over to the posters for *Mr Puntila and his Man Matti*, stuck up in glass display cases like menus. He examined the cast list and saw in small letters the name of Maria Eich in the role of Fina, the chambermaid. Did this mean that, from now on, she wouldn't be playing the big parts any more? He left the theatre and made his way to the banks of the Spree.

Between two poplar trees there was an old man who had spread out on a military blanket a few objects, a small clock, two men's watches from before the war, three bound volumes of Goethe, some combs and hairbrushes. And, instinctively, Hans wondered who this man, with his symmetrical features, looking as if he no longer expected anything from life, could be.

'What does it mean – a man? Before, you said you were a driver? I've caught you contradicting yourself...' In *Puntila*, someone said that, perhaps, indeed, Puntila himself. And Hans wondered whether he'd been a pharmacist? A head waiter? A wood merchant? He looked at this man between the poplars and reflected that poverty and war had reduced him to the state of a poplar. No more bitterness, but no more expectations either: the salt of humour and hope had dried everything up.

Hans Trow turned the Goethe volumes over in his hands, and sniffed at them to smell once more that odour of old paper and attics that evoked the pre-war years. A calm period, with something of the 19th century in its twilight, its silverware, its great austere families. He bought the volumes and threw in three coal vouchers. The man, amazed, didn't smile, and took forever to wrap up the volumes in an old piece of carefully smoothed butcher's paper...

Then, Hans walked down a few steps and sat down. His legs dangled over the Spree. He could hear a gurgling noise running along a pile of planks in a black hole of excavations. The disquieting, sunlit sadness of Berlin in the middle of summer...

He saw the figure of a young blond woman walk past, very quickly, up there, and was reminded of Maria. What had he gone and dragged her into? She was as respectful about her mission as she had doubtless been respectful during her catechism classes... but at bottom he knew nothing about her political opinions. Did she have any? She had only an 'pure and ardent heart', and basically she was the only person he didn't have any desire to gauge and manipulate. It was with the greatest reluctance that he asked her to photograph those bitter poems, that litany of disappointments that Brecht hid in a cupboard like a naughty boy.

Hans started to open the volumes of Goethe as he pondered the question of how to get Maria out of the Berliner Ensemble. The low noise of a trickle of water drew his attention. The only thing alive in this whole district, frozen in the sunlight, was this gurgle, the current of water running into a few planks and some decaying reeds.

Then he told himself that he loved Maria Eich, but this feeling was like an animal trapped in a cage, an antediluvian beast kept in a huge empty citadel. The minute he thought about this feeling of love, all he could see was his inability to transform it into action. He preferred to fail without even knowing why. He preferred a quick fuck here and there, a fling between two offices, the prostitutes in the outlying suburbs. It was strange to hoard a feeling of love, like an old man contemplating a small clock in a glass globe, pulling out a golden key so that he can carefully wind it up, hear it strike the hours, chiming, quivering in its tiny mechanism. He could hear Maria's heart chiming within him. Curiously, he wanted to keep Maria without touching her, simply never needing to spoil the love he felt for her. Not touching her.

'What's the remedy for that?' he thought.

Move away from the centre of the earthquake...

That's what he told himself, his jacket hanging over his shoulders: he had no desire to analyse his emotional deadlock. He had no desire to steal something from Maria and then to leave her short, as he'd done so often. The women he had loved, after all, had merely occupied subordinate posts in his life as an officer. Durability and balance were things he found only in his work and the discreet fears it aroused. He didn't want to make a grab at Maria and subject her to his ardour. Henceforth, his mission was to get her out of this Berlin trap, let her regain her freedom, somewhere else, in the other Germany or further away.

When he came back up to the poster outside the Deutsches Theater, he was, in the final analysis, glad to see Maria's name in small letters. She would return to anonymity.

12

Maria contravened her instructions. She left Brecht's office and cycled off to the village, saying she was going to get some milk. She made her way to the farmyard where she he had already come once before, then, as soon as her little jug of milk was full, she went to the post office. She propped her elbows on the wooden ledge in the telephone booth and waited for them to connect her to Berlin. She thought her heart was going to burst as she counted the seconds. Someone by the name of Karmitz arranged to meet her in an old abandoned Wehrmacht barracks near Prötzel, some twenty or so kilometres from Buckov. She jotted down his directions, and dropped her pen, and the brown envelope she was writing on.

After hanging up, she didn't move for a good five minutes, enough time to shake off her sense of oppression and calm down. Sweat was pouring from under her arms, her heart was thudding; she thought, 'A rabbit jumping into its hutch'. She brought her breathing under control and pushed open the door of the telephone booth that had enclosed the air soured by her fear.

Walk quietly along. Feel nice and steady on your legs. She heard insects buzzing in her left ear and wondered whether she wasn't succumbing to a brain tumour.

Finally, when she was sure that her heart wasn't going to burst in the post office, she forced herself to smile to the young woman behind the counter, telling her that Buckov was the prettiest area she had ever been in. The woman's incredulous face took Maria by surprise. She wondered if she wasn't arousing suspicion by feigning too great a cheerfulness in such a gloomy office.

Sturdy oaks, a patchily tarmacked road, little white-washed houses, birds flying up into a blue sky. And clear hills as far as the eye could see.

She followed the plan she had clumsily sketched out on the back of the envelope and found herself outside a group of buildings surrounded by barbed wire. There was a vast courtyard, slightly rounded, with cracks here and there. A large shed and, on the left, a concrete shelter with slits in the walls half-hidden by tall grass. The old barracks looked sinister, abandoned, strange in the middle of the countryside. The green horizon of the fields, the boundless sky, the clouds, and a few birds cheeping in the fruit trees.

Maria walked down a flight of stairs and reached a twilit room with lines of iron pillars. Long rows of tables, and benches stacked up. Hans Trow was waiting under the huge refectory clock. The daylight came in through the window and illumined his grey suit and his white open-necked shirt, immaculately ironed. He swung round to watch as Maria approached. He looked up in some embarrassment when she came up to him.

'Hallo, Hans,' she said, she thought, she repeated inside herself.

'I don't have much time,' said Hans.

'Give all of your time to me, me alone, I beg you,' thought Maria. She stood there awkwardly in front of him, with a passably solemn smile. He looks like an ordinary young man, but is there in this country a single ordinary man, pure of heart... in this country adrift...

'How are you?'

She can no longer grasp what she's hearing. Hans swings round, with a gentle, imperceptible smile. He asks her, as he jangles something metallic in his pocket, 'Why haven't you left for the West?'

He sits on a table corner.

'If you'd only asked me...'

'I'd have replied that you could leave.'

She shuddered, moved a step or two away, and her eyes fell on the obscene graffiti on the wall, blistered by the humidity. She felt void. A phantom. She folded her arms against her blouse. Hans Trow noticed that she was trembling. He came up to her and placed his hand on her shoulder.

'How are you feeling?'

'Not so good.'

She added, 'It often happens.'

Hans stared at her and the muscles round Maria's eyes quivered slightly. Hans didn't know what to do; he gently pulled on the straps of Maria's handbag and played with the little copper clasp, clicking it open and shut. Maria thought, 'Give me an island where I can love this man, any island; for me alone, this man, even if it's just for one week in my life...'

The long rows of tables emitted enough distress to fill an ocean. Maria's arms, so beautiful, hung at her sides. Hans was examining the photos, the prescriptions, the envelopes covered with little notes that Maria had jotted down in a spidery scrawl; they contained personal reflections, as well as the phrases seized on the wing when Brecht, after three schnapps, started to talk, in the evening, by the light of the candles.

'What's he done to you?'

'Nothing special.'

'Is he still thinking about China?'

'All the time.'

My God, she thought, let him take me, let him keep me, let him never go away... Never... My God, make him...

'I don't have much time, Maria, but you need to get to the West.'

Yes, Hans, fine, have you understood, Hans, that you must come with me?

'You are a rare type of person, Maria Eich, but you must leave; Communist surplus value is going to become something of only secondary importance, especially for someone like you. You're no longer up to it.'

She nearly said, 'I have a pure and ardent heart'.

Hans said, 'You can't be dependent on those people any more.'

He tried to find considerate, courteous, sincere turns of phrase to put an end to the distress of that gaze so close to him.

'You've succeeded to the full extent of your abilities, Maria.'

He held her by the wrist, the bag lay open between them on the table, she tried to lean against him more closely and this made her lose her balance. She buried her face in his jacket and stood immobile. The sweet, warm grass, pines and grass in our island, the two of us, one week, that's all I ask for, just one.

Hans gently detached himself and picked up the photos that lay scattered on the ground.

'You need to leave... When you come back to Berlin in September, you'll find your papers for the West, money, I'll take care of it all myself...'

She was a statue, with extraordinarily wide eyes. Her lower lip was trembling. He picked up the bundle of papers, and gave back her handbag, imbuing his gestures with as much courtesy and sensitivity as he could, but Maria seemed to be asleep, as if in a dream.

'Thank you,' she said, numbly.

'Don't thank me, Maria.'

They emerged into the yard. The harsh sunlight blinded them.

'Don't be sad,' he said. 'But we won't be seeing each other again.'

They walked along a sort swimming pool cemented with joints of tar. A black Soviet car was waiting, one of those big official cars forever crossing Berlin.

Hans opened the door and looked at Maria.

'Where are you going?'

'To get my bike.'

He is playing with the last drops of my blood and my life... How difficult and laborious it is, breathing. I'm going to die, thought Maria, her eyes misting over.

The windscreen turned in a flash of light then the car sped off behind the fence. No more island, no more perfumed gardens. Just an old wall, and windows covered with wire meshing. Maria had the sensation of being encircled in some immense landscape. Greenery that reflected no light. She pedalled along, weeping quietly and scrutinising, incredulously, the vast sky.

Give me a week on an island with him, a single day...

13

It's a jerky little film, whitish and streaky, with odd brown haloes slipping along the edge of the image. You can make out a rowing boat in the morning glitter of a lake. Black flickers on the left of the picture. Maria Eich is wearing huge dark glasses, a grey crew-neck pullover and a pair of baggy trousers that sometimes flap in the wind. Her face is framed by a headscarf.

Brecht, in his shirtsleeves, rows slowly. The boat glides over the lake in fits and starts. In the background, neat rows of birch trees. Brecht has put his cap back on. He rows with a weary, detached gesture while Maria Eich reads some sheets that seem to have the consistency of paper towels. It's not entirely clear why she is leaning in the shadow of the boat on the other side of the camera, but a commentary provided by Theo Pilla can be heard, somewhat faintly through the cracklings: 'After the billing and cooing phase, she's realised that the pig in his pigsty has only one idea in his head: to jump on top of her for a bit of bump and grind.'

In the monotonous depth of the silvery shadows, Maria's arm can be seen placing sheets of paper not back in the boat, but on the water. Someone asks, 'But what's she doing?' and in the tiny dry mechanical whirring of the projector, Hans Trow murmurs, 'Maria is avenging herself on Brecht by scattering his notes for a speech to the department of dramatic arts, and the lists of the new tasks of the theatre that the Lord and Master had churned out…'

'Do you have those notes?'

'We've got them. They were photographed by our agent directly from the master's typewriter.'

'Good,' interrupts a hoarse voice in the twilight, while they watch Brecht letting go of the oars, jumping up, losing his cap (it stays motionless on the water) and grabbing Maria Eich by the arm; she tries to hide the sheets behind her back. Pages flutter off in the sunlight, floating away from the boat, caught in the shimmer of the reeds. From the back of the room, someone is heard to murmur, 'You can leave that on my desk, the report. We'll send it to Moscow…'

The boat drifts along. Maria, having removed her glasses, smoothes the hair away from her face. Brecht is unfolding a sheet of water-sodden paper on the floor of the boat, crouching on all fours. Yes, Brecht is still trying to pick up the pages that float along like water lily flowers. Maria goes for a swim, enjoys herself. The gentle radiation of the shadow of the fir trees. Brecht picks up the oars while a young woman in a bathing costume disappears into the shadows. Standing erect, Brecht experiences the perplexity of a moment of emptiness. The landscape vibrates. Maria's head resurfaces in the glittering darkness and foliage of the landing. Maria's face, laughing, disappears again in the streaks of a sun-saturated image. The film breaks…

Later, when they got the projector working again, it was like another film. The sheets of paper had disappeared, nothing had taken place, the lake was again a mirror in the sunlight, empty, in the upper left-hand corner of the screen a woman was swimming. Then, framed in another shot, her black eyelashes became visible, still wet and tangled, and Hans said, 'This was filmed later in the day'.

The light was switched on to reveal a room full of uniforms.

Wilhelm Prachko, of group 4 of the Stasi, was listening to Hans Trow's report.

'Maria Eich performed in amusing little comedies in Vienna and isn't prepared for the stresses we have to live with. But she has regularly given us very reliable reports. She loathes Brecht's theory of drama that believes literature can be brought into the scientific era.'

Hans Trow added, 'She has always believed that theatre was no more than a series of magnetic passes, the art of a magician or a fakir... In that regard, she's simply a delightful Viennese actress from the end of the Empire, who expects love scenes, noble exploits, and the ardent sighs of a Prince Charming.'

There was some further discussion of the slow and gruelling procedures for the pensions to be paid to veterans of the war in Spain. The uniforms all stood up and left the room, chattering.

'Where is she?' interrupted Wilhelm Prachko.

'In her apartment in Schumannstrasse,' said Hans Trow.

'Take care of her.'

14

On the day before his autumn return to Berlin, Brecht had gone out before daybreak. The lake was grey and dreary. The mist was clearing, the pines came into view. Brecht watered the rose bushes. Dressed in his crumpled old mac, and his worn-out beach sandals, he put down the watering can. He gazed at the lake.

Helene appeared, coming down the steps of the big house. She was carrying a pile of clothes.

'Already up?'

'Couldn't sleep…'

'Me neither.'

'I was wondering how to tell Maria certain things…'

She brought over two cups and the coffee.

'If you don't know how to say them, don't say them.'

They drank.

'She's not really had any training.'

'She does have charm.'

'Hmm,' sighed Helene Weigel, 'who doesn't?'

'She has a certain… inner beauty…'

Her tiny bracelets tinkled together as she put in the sugar.

'Can't say I'd noticed.'

They walked as far as the pavilion, arm in arm.

'She's finally realised she's not up to it.'

'High time.'

'She does have a certain something.'

Silence. Brecht sat on the steps and pulled his cap right down over his nose.

'I can't just merrily get rid of her.'

'Well keep her then! You can scratch her head for her. In any case, you scratch her head exactly the same way you did with that mongrel Wriccles in Santa Monica.'

'She was made for Broadway. A bright young thing, just perfect for a petty-bourgeois theatre.'

At five past nine, Maria came out in a white blouse with blue spots and a splendid pair of khaki shorts that hugged her figure really fetchingly. She stuck a daisy in her hair.

She sat at the garden table. Brecht was reading the coffee and tin prices in an American newspaper. He was gently grousing. He had discovered that the coffee-producing countries could sell to only four or five buyers worldwide, who paid prices that were much too low. And yet his morning coffee was disgusting.

He told her a strange story about a couple to explain to her what he meant by the 'alienation effect'. A certain woman's egotism threatened to drain her husband's strength and stop him doing his job. So the husband took the decision to escape from her influence. But the whole art of conjugal life consists in not making too much of a fuss about this decision. Remaining fresh, available, attentive, lovable. The more the decision to escape from the woman became self-obvious and implacable, the more the man forced himself to think nice things about the young woman. But he had to do it in an objective and thus distanced or 'alienated' way, as you do for people who are not particularly close to you. Instead of getting angry at her whims, the husband imposed on himself the task of justifying them and approving of them. Brecht added, 'There's nothing more difficult than leaving someone without running them down'.

'Are you saying that for me?'

Halfway through the morning, Brecht leafed through a volume of Shakespeare's sonnets.

Then he went to join Maria who, with an inexpressive face, was staring at the shimmering lake over there.

'All right?'

'Not really.'

He didn't persist.

At noon, at the dinner table, everyone talked about the performances in Berlin that had not met with a particularly warm response in the press. There was a silence. Wasps swarmed around the fruit bowl.

In the afternoon, Maria packed her bag and took advantage of Ernst Busch's car to return to Berlin.

15

There was a weekend of mist. Berlin in a yellow soup. Everything became skeletal, branches, masses, steam, smoke, a watery impregnation, fluttering wings, creaking lines, haloes, enormous and diffuse tremulous masses that grazed you as you passed. For two afternoons, Maria heard Brecht talking about Karl Valentin, that scrawny comedian who had taught the young man from Augsburg so much about mime, then there were endless rehearsals of a fishwives' squabble. Brecht concluded from all this: We shed tears over our clowns, we laugh until our sides split at our tragedians, petty-bourgeois feeling is the measure of all things, in short, nothing has changed, every thing is possible, unfortunately...

Then there was blue sky on Wednesday. Her telephone line was cut and Maria had the feeling that her apartment had been visited; she found in her dressing room quite an old issue of *Neues Deutschland* that mentioned the denazification trials and, curiously, there were the names of her husband and father on page four, carefully folded at just the right place. Who had come into her dressing room to slip the paper there?

She went out to post a birthday telegram to her daughter who'd just turned six. Damp alleyways. A little shop with hardboard panels instead of real window panes, seemingly abandoned. There was a big white cat all covered in dust stretched on old bound copies of Shakespeare's plays. The white cat looked up and its eyes followed the scraps of paper whirling round in the alleyway. Maria entered the shop to buy the books, but they were too expensive and she reflected that she would like to have given these volumes as a present, not to Brecht, but to Hans Trow, though that was quite senseless. The memory of the cat watching the papers whirling round stayed with her for several days. A sign of her frivolity. She heard patriotic songs as she walked past a secondary school, *Germany, United Fatherland… may the sun shine over Germany…* and so on and so forth, then she crossed a kind of rampart of concrete behind which Soviet uniforms were having their photos taken.

In the evening, she slipped into a long blue-mauve dress with spangles, put on some lipstick, painted her fingernails, put on court shoes, took her pearl necklace out of a velvet case and made her way to a grand reception at Pieck's where they were going to award Hans Eisler, the official musician, with a decoration.

When she climbed up the steps to the main entrance and saw all those bureaucrats, Maria felt ill at ease; she was offered a glass of champagne. She took it with her past the picture window from which she could see a parade ground. There were buildings painted a dull yellow, lit by high steel towers from which a cone of drizzle seemed to swirl down.

It was rumoured that the new State Security services had moved in there, as well as the training services for the teachers People's Police schools. She felt buried in yet another umpteenth year of the war, swallowed up in an endless winter, a universe of uniforms, a universe of avenues covered with rubble that resembled ashes, a universe in which everything that composed civilian life, the orders, the toasts to peace and friendship between fraternal peoples, the security services' rubber stamps, the signatures, the special mentions – all of this was no longer a transitional stage they were momentarily obliged to get through, but the inevitable law of a world of fear, of endless migration, in which everything looked and felt like a canteen for starving populations. Everywhere, she said to herself, we have to paddle through mud and ruins, informing on one another. She saw stretching out before her a black country of mica and frozen crystals, a world built of planks, sacks of cement, caught amid barking dogs, wire netting, abandoned apartment blocks, in the middle of a time that never ceased to swirl around you and from which you would never awaken.

This world was gurgling in the endless rain, in the endless poverty of slogans. A world of government stooges and robots, endless trials, reports, commissions, obligatory signatures, *Volkspolizei*, teaching skills forever being evaluated, instructions, police rules and regulations, unmasked plots, legal emotions, military parades, young people's assemblies, a universe of spades, pickaxes, ballast, forced labour, inspections and convictions ceaselessly asserted, blue shirts and blouses, children lined up in rows, Maria couldn't take any more. She wanted an island, the sea a deep green, all the water of a huge wave that would cover them all, the great waters of the equinox sweeping them away, the great swells of the ocean in which she could forget.

The uniformed soldiers formed a kind of shadow around her, a vague murmur. There was talk of musical culture, of article 6, of incitements to boycott on the part of the West.

To dragoon, conclude, triumph. Endless mass demonstrations, speeches from the podium, releases of doves, slogans bellowed out, grandiloquent declarations in the newspapers, tracts, political cant, the extermination of the bourgeois class, tables surrounded by men in grey suits, the labelling of antisocial elements to be eliminated, entire classes of teenagers haltingly reciting optimistic poems, framed photos of Stalin or Wilhelm Pieck. This was the world she moved in.

Those women in long skirts parading by with a forest of placards. In tight blouses, they continued to repeat optimistic slogans. Maria kept her distance from anyone who, at official gatherings, spoke in low tones of the people who had made dubious compromises with the petty bourgeoisie of the West, and from all those Party members who walked across the courtyard strewn with dead leaves and pointed out the rooftops of the West, shining in the rain as if giant spiders were scuttling across them. She no longer replied to those who placed themselves at the service of a single idea that distorted all their judgements. She remained mute when faced with those Party members, thickset, in shirtsleeves, with wide braces, who lolled in the armchairs of the Seagull Club and repeated songs from their Communist youth. She avoided those who publicly sided with a political position that for fifteen years had not been theirs. All of this troubled her, gnawed away at her. She kept asking herself so many questions, she felt alone, defenceless against Weigel and Brecht – he now used his talent for mockery solely to keep at bay those people forever asking him why he was sacrificing his talent to a false official virtue. All those people who wanted their attitude to be exemplary and who sacrificed their sensibility, their art, their delicacy to the pitiless political interests of the moment. She couldn't take any more.

East Berlin
1952

Early in the morning
The fir trees are of copper.
I saw them looking like that
Half a century
And two world wars ago,
With young eyes.

Bertolt Brecht

I

Captain Alan Croyd had a corner office on the second floor of one of those villas that line the Richterstrasse. From the picture window there was a superb view over an old race course. It had become a training ground for the marines and a supply centre for barrels of petrol. On the old Hebbel stadium, the joint allied headquarters had installed a supply centre with tarred-roof huts, full of essential items for the population of Berlin in the case of a long blockade.

The villa next door with its brown cement and its eastern-style balconies harboured all the electro-optical ironmongery of the CIA.

The old residence of the Hardenberg princes was occupied by the archive services of General Stanley Bay. It contained all the intelligence literature kept by officers who were now more or less retired and only ever read the sports pages of the *New York Times* and all the propaganda issued by the politicians in Pankow. Behind them, telexes were rattling away in a bluish light, bringing news from the head office in Washington DC. A man in white overalls walked over at regular intervals to tear off the long strips of paper that spooled endlessly out onto the lino. In the grey-walled room on the other side of the corridor, brown magnetic tapes turned slowly; the upper part of this small room was crammed with metallic drawers in which were filed every negative of every aerial photograph of all the air raids which, from Hamburg to Dresden, had reduced Germany to a series of coastal strips over which flew flocks of wild geese.

Alan Croyd was conscientiously examining Maria Eich's file surrounded by bundles of paperwork, under a blue steel lamp that shed its light on the entry vouchers for the tennis club at HQ. The cone of light from the office lamp fell on an adjacent note from the British secret services in Vienna based in the Kohlmarkt.

Captain Alan Croyd was absorbed in such a profound meditation that he seemed almost asleep. The creased blue note with its traces of carbon paper trembled slightly in his left hand. This austere man with his greying hair looked up at Maria. A vague whiff of cigar rose from an iron box depicting an old sailor surrounded by sperm whales, a box of dull metal that must have been scratched with a penknife. There was also an English-German conversation manual published in Zurich in 1933 and a red diplomatic service card.

Croyd resumed the conversation in a kindly, weary tone of voice, as if this were a mere routine preliminary to something else.

'What did you talk about with Brecht?'

'Nothing serious.'

'You mean nothing political?'

'No, just nothing.'

'But there were serious conversations in your presence? Political conversations?'

'Yes, with Helene Weigel, with assistants, theatre directors.'

'But not with you?'

'No, with me the talk was all... pretty frivolous...'

'For instance?'

'My make-up, my legs.'

'You were his... his... girlfriend... Is that right?...'

'I don't know... For a long time I thought so... not in the last few months...'

'What did he have to say about us Americans?'

'Hollywood had left him with some bad memories... He said that... I remember he often said that the Americans and the English didn't know how to "earthify" artistic experience. They kept dragging the Bible in... and the new theatre, he said, needs to "demetaphysicise everything".'

'Did you know he'd been asked to appear before the Committee on UnAmerican Activities?'

'Yes.'

'Had he become a member of the Communist Party?'

'I don't think so...'

'Did he ever mention Joe Forster to you?'

'No.'

Croyd jotted down a few words in a blue notebook bedecked with the emblem of the American eagle. Then he put his pencil down and smiled at Maria. He started to open some drawers.

'Did he mention the possible purchase of a house in Switzerland?'

'Never.'

'Did he have money on him?'

'A little.'

'You're not sure about that?'

'No…'

'Did he suggest you leave the Berliner Ensemble?'

'No.'

'Did he suggest you move to West Berlin, and in particular the American Sector?'

'No.'

'Who did suggest it?'

'Nobody.'

'And what are you going to do?'

'Give German lessons in a Catholic institute near the Goethe-Park.'

'Were the members of the Cultural Commission worried about the "artistic" programmes' (he stumbled over the word 'artistic') 'of Bertolt Brecht?'

'He had a special status…'

'Everyone was spying on everyone else…'

'Maybe… I don't know…'

A woman who worked for the service, in uniform, brought a tray with a teapot in faded yellow metal, sugar lumps set out on a saucer and two tall whitish-yellow beakers.

'Did he go to Moscow?'

'No. I don't think so.'

Captain Croyd's questions created the impression that he was encouraging her to reveal nothing essential, as if, in any case, Brecht's slightest movements, and the affairs of the Berliner Ensemble, had all been known for so long that all they needed were a few details to fill in the paperwork and give it, if not a final polish, at least a semblance of precision.

'Where are you staying?'

'In a small furnished house, not far from St Thomas's. The Adler Hotel.'

Then, there was an endless, tedious conversation about Maria's husband and father and their respective disappearances; the Captain indulged in a bit of bluff when he made out that he had a message to pass on to them, in an attempt to find out once and for all whether Maria was in touch with them. Eventually, Croyd seized a pair of Ray-Bans lying on his desk, contemplated the lenses and said, 'You spied for that agent... you lied for him, practically risked your neck for him – who was he, Trow?'

Maria didn't reply.

'Well, come on, tell me.'

'A decent guy. He was doing the same work as you.'

'Really?'

'Yes.'

'Really!'

Faced with Maria's stubborn silence, Croyd rose to his feet, or, rather, unfolded himself. He busied himself with a little tape recorder and its transparent spools that seemed to fill a transparent thread with their glow. The spools stopped.

'Did you keep the camera that you used for...'

'No.'

The fact of the matter was, thought Croyd, that this actress probably was imbued with a certain patriotic fervour, more interesting than a mere instinct for self-preservation. Several times Croyd glanced at Maria who was slipping on her grey-black coat with its round collar, but that delicate face was impassive. Croyd decided that, in the final analysis, it was perhaps the nape of her neck that was the most alluring... He accompanied her back into the corridor, in a sombre mood.

The weather hung drearily over this vast desert with its building sites, military huts, construction work and old cobbled yards. In the afternoon he would have to compose a few telegrams and see if the army typing pool had completed the correct files.

2

In the following months, Maria Eich was summoned to see Croyd six times. The third time, he touched her arm. In general when he asked her questions he would turn his back on her and gaze out at the network of clouds that, in Berlin, extended particularly far once the morning mists had evaporated.

The lights came on around six in the evening; they seemed, as if by miracle, to come to a halt along a pine wood; that was the Soviet zone. The cold breath of another Berlin... One day, the CIA would transform the air currents in the sky and the highest winds and turn them upside down and shed a sort of glacial rain so as to drown the building sites, the encampments, the children in the streets, the Soviet soldiers playing chess in front of the windows with their smashed stained glass...

At the third interrogation, Croyd put down his notebook, and disconnected the tape recorder. A shaft of sunlight through the clouds lit up the immensity of Berlin; he opened the picture window. The distant murmur of the district could be heard, then the echo of voices in an enclosed courtyard.

Maria was trying to explain that her husband had been a Nazi, and her father a friend of Rudolf Hess, and that he had always rejoiced at the sight of the German tank units plunging into the whiteness of the Russian deserts, rejoiced at the sight of thousands of Stukas invading the European skies, been delighted at this grand confrontation that would finally provide living space for an Aryan populace which had imagined the future in such grandiose style.

'I even heard him singing as he pushed his bike down the garden path the day Hitler gave his speech at the Heldenplatz.'

'And that didn't bother you?'

'I never read a newspaper all the way through. Just the theatre pages... and the horoscope...'

'And Brecht? Why did you like him so much?'

'No, I didn't like him. I admired him.'

'Okay, let's begin at the beginning: who put you in touch with him?'

She told him. The feeling that her whole generation had been trampled underfoot by the Nazis and that they'd all been so thoroughly indoctrinated. You don't come across that many real geniuses.

'What are you getting at?'

'Brecht is a real genius.'

She started to wax enthusiastic. Her cheeks flushed. She talked about his songs, his poems, the house painter.

'What house painter?'

'Brecht called Hitler the house painter, from 1930 onwards.'

'Why? *Was* he a house painter?'

This observation indicated a strange lack of intelligence or, at least, experience – a very poor knowledge of the Hitler file.

This reassured Maria.

'Do you know the *Song of the SA Man*?' she asked ironically. 'The *Song of the Class Enemy*? Do you know *In Praise of Dialectics*? And the *Ballad of the World's Approval*? Would you like me to sing them for you?'

Feeling she was scoring points, Maria continued.

'Do you know *The Late Lamented Fame of the Giant City of New York*?' she added.

When Croyd expressed surprise, she started to recite, very loud: 'Specimens of humanity, who were penned up together in great enclosures, who were given special food, and bathed, and made to swing to and fro, so that their incomparable movements could be recorded on film for all future generations'.

There was a moment of embarrassment.

'Thank you,' said Croyd.

He dropped the tea bag into his cup. He found it rather sad that this little actress endowed with such a pretty body should still be set ablaze by her old alchemist Brecht, and yet at the same time he was fascinated by this young woman's acid charm. She became quite radiant when she hummed. Deep down, thought Croyd, she agrees with what they're doing. Completely on their side.

He pulled the tea bag out of his cup. A tall, slender secretary brought a half-sheet of blue paper on which had been written, 'Your wife telephoned from New York'.

Croyd tapped his thin lips pensively without listening to what Maria was saying.

'What about his political commitments?' asked Croyd, clearing his throat.

At this question, Maria suffered a mental block. She lifted her gaze to Croyd. He was thinking of 'those adorable curly-haired little Viennese women who devour strudels while humming *Così fan tutte* as they shake their brooms out of the window'.

He tried to help her; but inspiration failed him. He told himself he had all the time in the world to bring her in again. And he used one of his favourite phrases.

'You don't give me any cause for complaint. Thank you for your full and frank cooperation.'

From this third floor, with its extensive view across Berlin, you can sense Time's heavy and hopeful breath. It drags along in its wake this city made up of never-ending hassle, barbed wire fences, the flights of wild ducks, bells, gleaming sunlight, microphones, building sites, pitted facades, and brutalised writings. Letters of stone. Dusty printing works. Sheds.

At six in the evening, the secretary brought another cup of warm water. He dangled his tea bag over the cup. In the same way, he holds the thread of the lives of those he interrogates. For a moment, he is irradiated by the city's morbid grandeur and the power that his official ribbons confer on him over those who come to sit in front of his desk, facing a photographic enlargement of the American sector.

The tea bag falls into the cup.

3

In June '53, she learnt from the papers of the revolt in East Berlin. On 17th June, the workers had demonstrated in the streets against the reduction in their wages that had been decreed by the Politburo. Maria went up onto the terrace roof of the Adler Hotel and watched the smoke rising from the northern districts. She learnt that Soviet tanks had taken up positions at all the major crossroads in East Berlin and that Lavrenti Beria, the powerful head of the Soviet police, had come over urgently from Moscow and ordered the Soviet troops to be ready to intervene while, in the Western sector, the French, English and American occupation armies were also in a state of alert, ready to move in. Brecht, who was rehearsing *Don Juan*, spoke to his actors about what was happening even as gunfire and flames were filling the district with smoke. That same evening, he decided to compose a letter of support to Ulbricht's government.

Then, a few days later, the streets were clear again. Silence. Sunlit cobbles. Sparrows.

The newspapers in the West published the letter that Brecht had addressed to Comrade Ulbricht: 'I feel the need, at this moment, to tell you of my allegiance to the Unified Communist Party of Germany'. It was insinuated that the Pankow government had blue-pencilled the rest of the letter, in which Brecht had been more critical. In the hotel, Brecht's letter was discussed without anyone knowing that Maria had been his mistress.

As she crossed the porch of the institute where she taught, every morning, Maria had to make an effort not to feel giddy, since she was well aware that her position, which consisted in revealing her relationship with Brecht to Croyd, resembled her own life – an eternal betrayal. But of what? Of whom? And why?

Winter came. Imagine an evening that sets in quickly and makes you think of tombs. A flight of crows. A lake that is grey and then black. Fetch your coat out of the cupboard.

In November, a white helmet of the Military Police appeared, framed by the cathedral glass of the entrance hall. He was bringing a new summons to the joint allied HQ. The man, Harold Gray, stepped into the halo of light shed from the outside lamp; he had something rather stiff in his manner. As she returned to the dining room, Maria again felt threatened. One of the hotel boarders asked her, 'Bad news?'

'Oh no,' she said, 'just routine.'

That night, she had a dream. She again saw the white helmet of the Military Police coming up to the entrance hall. There was a silence. Then Maria opened the door and it wasn't an American soldier but a cordial SA, holding in one hand a bottle of beer and in the other a summons. And the SA entered the hotel, watching Maria who was scurrying round in a panic trying to find her coat and gloves, and he said to her, 'no need to get panicky, grandma... It's just a simple summons for you to come and have a meal of goose with us! A matinal-socialist goose. You'll see, it tastes just as nice!... Just as nice as before the war!'

Then Maria Eich woke up. She half-opened the French window that looked out over the balcony. Berlin lay there, calm, luminous, vaguely twinkling. She told herself that over on the other side of the city, Brecht was asleep. He had witnessed Hitler's debut in Munich. Brecht had walked through the streets where all that had happened. Brecht knew how very effective Nazi dramaturgy, and Nazi theatricality, with its torch-lit retreats, its big words, its huge parades, its songs, its banners, its wakes, had been. What a theatre of sheer effectiveness they had been, those Nazi ceremonies! Big words, big platforms, the mosaics of men with radiant faces, the very same men who had been poor, jobless vagabonds... Brecht knew how this dramatic setting had filled the German people with such enthusiasm. Yes, Hitler had been better at stage-craft than he had. Bertolt certainly had something to worry about – he'd spent all his years in exile trying to work out how the 'emotional extortion racket' of fascism could have worked so well, filling the crowds with pleasure and sweeping them up with it.

How had that pure theatre so successfully wooed the crowds? What dialectical intelligence, what new kind of theatre needed to be established in opposition to that fascist, Wagnerian theatricality?

Brecht had mulled over this question all his life long and today he was sitting in an official stand and watching model little girls parading by in their blue skirts and white blouses.

Alone under the moon, Maria Eich thought it over. In the gleam of the local streetlights, everything was quiet, everything was getting a few hours' sleep. And yet, there was a mysterious subdued buzz. 'What if it were all to begin again tomorrow?' Maria thought. Would Brecht and his friends, would their irony, their refined intelligence be enough?

It was Brecht who had told Maria, 'Man lives from the products of his head but it isn't much. Try it and see: the most that lives off *your* head is a louse.'

Maria contemplated the big villas nearby, swathed in the moonlight. She felt that her fear had not dissolved. She had lost all optimism.

4

Croyd was examining yet again Maria Eich's file surrounded by the paperwork piled round his type-writer.

Yet again, Maria noted the huge contrast between the coarsely dyed and recut uniforms of the East German police, and these impeccable American shirts. There was even a pair of sunglasses laid on the metal desk. The shirtsleeves rustled on the chrome chair, the fingers leafed through a file... The subtle interweaving of inks of different colours made you think of a medieval illumination rather than a document. But what amazed her, in this jumble of papers, was the apparition of a half-faded swastika rubber stamp.

Suddenly, Croyd lowered his head, reread a few lines through narrowed eyes and pulled out of his drawer a yellow, serrated photograph.

'Do you recognise him?'

A young man with a forage cap leaning against the turret of a Tiger tank, smoking a cigarette, smiling boyishly.

'Yes, he's my husband,' she said.

'Sorry?' he said.

'He's my husband,' she forced herself to say.

Croyd picked up the photo and examined it.

'He was a real fucking Nazi...'

Maria noticed that a new type of tape recorder was turning. She understood why they were making her repeat everything.

'Do you recognise him?'

'Yes,' said Maria. 'He's my husband!'

'He was.'

Croyd handed her another photo.

'They've found him dead in Portugal…'

'Pardon?'

'He was in charge of a dried fish cannery at Nazaré'.

'Where?' she asked.

'Portugal… Nazaré…'

He pushed three gleaming photos in front of Maria. A heavy shape, caught in the flash, a door opening onto the toilets. A flush with a length of string instead of a chain, something that looked like a shelf with cleaning products and, above all, the body bizarrely twisted, a medallion and a half-bearded face.

Croyd's propelling pencil crossed out a word on the back of a photo.

'Do you recognise him?'

'Yes,' said Maria. 'How did he die?'

'We don't know. Are you shocked?' he asked.

'Yes,' said Maria.

Croyd said, 'He'd done quite a few disgusting things, in Hungary and other places, did you know that?'

The spools of the tape recorder continued to turn, shuddering slightly.

She knew that he had drawn up lists and had 'terrorists' shot.

She wondered where Nazaré was, how it was possible to die there. Was it an exquisite little Portuguese fishing village of the kind you see on post cards? Or quite the opposite, a dismal place, a flat, muddy stretch of coast with gorse bushes and sheds filled with the stench of fish?

Croyd seemed to be waiting in some embarrassment. As if he had a clock in his head and just a few seconds to grant to Maria's distress, then, after that, tennis, the swimming pool, reports, phone calls he needed to make...

'Will his body be brought home?' asked Maria.

'He's buried in Nazaré...'

'Ah...'

The rain was starting to stream down the picture window. It was drowning the city.

Maria placed her hand on the edge of the table, at the very moment when Croyd stood up and turned off the lamp. The interview was over. He saw her out into the corridor. The lino made his crepe soles swish. Like a detached echo of himself. She held tight to a guardrail.

Croyd was starting to offer her his condolences but he was interrupted by an orderly who brought him a garment bag and his tennis racket.

She went downstairs without taking the lift. The steps of travertine were nice and clean and her heels clattered down them. It was the same on the other floors. A great enterprise, functioning smoothly amid the telephone calls, the doors nonchalantly pushed open with a foot, the rubbish bins covered with stencilled inscriptions.

5

They were sitting in the Walter-Ulbricht stadium.

Hans Trow observed Theo Pilla as he tried to slip a shiny green lettuce leaf between two slices of bread with a hard-boiled egg filling.

'Are you sure we mightn't have needed that... Maria Eich... now Brecht is dead, she could tell us a thing or two, couldn't she?'

'No.'

'You sure?'

'Yes.'

Hans Trow added, 'We didn't need her any more'.

'We never did need her.'

'We did!'

'You're taking the piss.'

'No,' said Hans.

'You were hurt when she cleared off to the Yanks!... drinking coke...'

'Yes.'

'There's one point I'd like to clear up before I leave for Moscow,' said Theo. 'I'd like to know if you really were in love with her.'

'Yes.'

'I was sure of it.'

Theo finished his rye bread sandwich feeling reconciled with the world. It was always like that when he ate, he could put the bottomless pits of sadness and the ultimate questions behind him. They left the stands and walked down the cinder track.

'Tell me,' he continued, 'there's one more point I'd like to clear up.'

'Yes.'

'Were you always in love with her?'

'Yes.'

'But, with her, did you…'

'No.'

'Never?'

'No.'

They left the stadium and walked to the tram stop.

Hans looked at his watch and pulled up the collar of his gabardine. Another seven minutes. The tram would be packed with workers.

Inside, they were squeezed quite close together. Hans leant over and murmured to Theo, 'Now stop stirring up memories, and don't put any sugar in your coffee in Moscow, okay? I don't want you ever to mention Maria Eich's name again…'

They separated at Alexanderplatz, Hans left line 3 on foot and headed to the avenue in the park where he had seen Maria for the last time without her seeing him. Here silence reigned, and building materials, coal, fences, huts. The dragging steps of a sentinel guarding a storage tank. He made his way to the Spree riverside. He walked for a long time along the water, past the giant steel gates of a complex, and went into a café, the Buffalo Café. He drank three beers and a schnapps; feeling much brighter, he walked into the shade of the next bridge.

6

In summer 1954, diplomatic notes were exchanged between the German Federal Republic and the German Democratic Republic and a prohibited zone (Sperrzone) established all along the border between them.

Maria grew worried. With her daughter, she got into the inter-zone train that was so often inspected. Two suitcases and the address that a teacher had given her. She was to make her way to Pforzheim, in Baden Württemburg, where there was a Catholic institute that needed a German teacher.

She climbed into one of those brown, rather grubby compartments with her daughter, who soon went off to sleep, and crossed Germany with its peaceful hills, its huge, flat, gently undulating fields; as the sun set they passed woods, military defences, encampments, pillboxes. Her passport was regularly checked by men in grey macs and brown hats. Then there were searchlights, more pillboxes, American and English uniforms, passport controls, luggage inspections... Maria saw her Berlin past disappearing just as her Viennese past had done. Ravines and hills, bridges, rivers, ruins.

She had the feeling, under the pale skies of Düsseldorf, that she was finally going to rid herself of any desire to live. She was leaving any longing for recognition behind her in Berlin. She would abdicate her old self and meld into the anonymity of the crowds.

She watched the landscape floating by; it resembled her. Bracken as far as the eye could see, dark forests. From now on, her secret and her anonymity would become her travelling companions. She would look after herself and her daughter with patience and common sense.

She was absorbed in this kind of thought when she arrived at the Cologne station. She took another train, smaller, narrow, with creaking woodwork. Her heart was tense, a captive heart, no longer an ardent heart. She reached the town of Pforzheim in the middle of tranquil little valleys. She felt herself coming back to life in the forested landscape.

January passed by, February, March, April. Windy weather, clear weather. She settled down in a handsome grey house built in the thirties, with a wooden balcony that overlooked the residential district. A feeling of gratitude. She could hear the bells of a church. She had a small garden. She easily adapted to her life as a teacher. Long vacations. Lotte was growing. Maria bought a second-hand Opel. She would go for long drives down those smooth, damp Black Forest roads, to Schellbronn, Badliebenzell, Calw, Wildberg, Nagold. She sometimes even went as far as Tübingen. There she was filled with fervour when she saw the tower where the poet Hölderlin had lived his years of madness, tribute, and ceremony. She no longer felt imprisoned, not by anything. She did not have to await the applause of the audience. She no longer concealed her face behind a mask of greasepaint. She was not haunted by the idea she needed to build up a character; she was no longer tense with panic when she walked down the stairs, from the wings onto the stage...

At the institute, she would avoid personal conversations. She only ever talked about the weather, the showers, the snow, the migrating clouds, the sudden cold snaps, the first hot spells, deck-chairs and candle-lit evenings. They considered her to be passive and a bit dumb; her lessons proved the opposite. She was attentive, precise, amusing, and ironic with her pupils. She told them more about the poets Heine and Hölderlin than about the prose writers. She always wore the same old black and white pullover, and a grey skirt. According to certain of her colleagues, she gave off a whiff of something 'halfway between chastity and the smell of chlorine in swimming pools'.

She rarely made any comment on events, except on 14th August 1961, when the Soviets started to unroll the barbed wire and install *chevaux de frise,* requisitioned masons and walled over the apartment windows. Berlin was being split in two. She remarked on this event with some brutality. This 'society fed off death; the darkness there was endless, limitless, and would never finish'.

She seemed elusive and almost mute. In the summer, she would swim in a pool in Wildbach. Children as well as women sunned themselves round the water. They were fascinated by the whiteness of her back, the regular movements of her arms, the fluid line of her legs, the fine wake of bubbles that accompanied her feet. Her white, narrow back gleamed resplendent when she emerged into the broad noonday sunlight, near the diving-board, to rub herself dry. She was remarkable, beautiful, absent.

The wooded residential district in which she lived suited her. With its calm, massive houses, its well-kept gardens, its rustic hills and dales, and its streets at right angles, it gave off a feeling of serenity. The only thing that disturbed the tranquillity of this district was the American Starfighters flying over. Metallic reflections, skimming the fir trees in a roar that was soon absorbed by the clouds. Then all that was left was the silence, the neighbour's hedge, the deck-chairs, Lotte's bike propped against the garden gate.

The publication of Brecht's complete works in the Suhrkamp edition was something Maria took the greatest interest in. She leafed through the heavy volumes and bought them. Her years as an actress passed before her eyes. There was no mention of her in the notes; she was relieved.

She kept a secret love, Hans Trow by name. She realised as much one evening when she was reading *Zeit* magazine on the banks of the Neckar. On page eight there was a photo of several uniformed police-men, Vopos. They had discovered the entrance to a tunnel in East Berlin, in a restaurant cellar. There was the face of a man in grey civilian clothes and Maria unerringly recognised Hans Trow, his expression of curiosity, the somewhat receding shape of his chin, his faint smile. Her stomach contracted. She felt the nape of her neck grow stiff. She felt like cotton wool, her mouth went dry. The afternoon was dark, shapeless, terrible, the evening endless and desolate. She walked past the houses in the district then climbed the bluish hills, but nothing saved her from her sorrow. Her legs followed the shadows. In a single instant she had lost her habits, her thoughts, the sense of confidence she had laboriously regained here, with her solitary walks, her hours spent swimming, her excursions by car down the roads; it was all smashed to pieces.

Eventually she took refuge in a pub. She drank. To loosen the grip on her, the pain. But there had been, hidden deep inside her for so long, a prayer that had never been answered, a prayer from which nothing more could be expected.

In the following weeks, she paid more sustained attention to her pupils' work. In the evening, she listened eagerly to what Lotte was telling her about her final school exams.

In August of the next year, Maria took her daughter to an island in the North Sea, Borkum. She stayed in a small hotel with full board, the Grafwaldersee. The two women were joined by a tall blond schoolboy, Stefan, who had also passed his exams with flying colours. He flirted with Lotte.

A blue sky, low winds, great banks of cloud sweeping by, and huge waves that reminded her of other summers without her trying to identify them.

Maria leafed through the newspapers, piles of them, German and Austrian papers. The Berlin Wall had had a strange influence on Maria's way of thinking. Instead of rejecting Marxism, she took an interest in it the way some people take an interest in phylloxera or gangrene. She felt inhibiting forces working within her, a bizarre state of psychological fermentation. She couldn't manage to imagine the lives of other people. She spent her days staring fixedly at families, wondering at the way human beings wove bonds with one another. How could anyone be married? How could anyone speak, be silent, sleep with someone, talk nonsense, play cards, do business?

She examined the tables full of young people in front of the cafes, a man whistling to his dog, a couple of ladies wearing hats advancing along the dike holding each other tight. Yes, she was dumbstruck by the spectacle of everyday life.

When she returned to Pforzheim at the end of August, she found the same house, with its empty corridors, the garden glittering and calm, the green plants. So hadn't her absence changed anything?

One evening, through the open window, where she'd hung up a thin net curtain to keep out the flies, she heard a couple passing by. The man was talking in a low voice. She was touched.

The days, like the nights, were regular, infinite, monotonous, silent. Maria would put her sports bag on the lawn, slip into her swimming costume, and dive into the Wildbach swimming pool. She glided under the water so as not to disturb the shadows and the reflections.

One Sunday evening, feeling a bit fed up, she picked up her flat key, climbed into her Opel, and headed in the direction of the institute where she taught. She opened the front door, her feet walked through the dry leaves that were strewn across the yard. Scaffolding had been put up along staircase B. She entered a long entrance hall with its row of brass coat hooks. In her class, all she could see were the tubular tables. Her umbrella was there, propped against the cupboard. The shadow from the window fell across a map of the world. She looked at the empty school seats in their tidy rows. There were only ghosts, the ghosts of pupils, a whole throng of ghosts.

On the blackboard there were drawings of little trees and a huge sun. Someone had tried to write his first name backwards: samoh… for Thomas, perhaps. There was also a box of chalks filled with chalk dust and scissors with rounded points.

She was keenly susceptible to the odour of oblivion, and contemplated, with emotion, the dusty portraits of Goethe and Jean-Jacques Rousseau. Everything seemed abandoned, everything had been just left there, summer was turning into autumn.

She walked over to the spot, near the radiator, where she would regularly take up position during written exams. From here, you could look right down into the schoolyard. The day was already starting to wane. She could see the bright twinkling of the city lying down below, a few blocks of business offices, the hazy brightness that lay over the whole district, the first neon lights coming on.

An incredible tranquillity reigned. The whole school was motionless, dark, vast, empty, strange, unreal. Maria found it calming. A window had been left open, the rain started to patter down into the yard. Water poured from a drainpipe higher up. But here, in this classroom, you were sheltered from the violence outside, the propaganda, the Starfighters, and the diplomatic notes from Moscow.

She stood for a long while contemplating the dictionaries, the encyclopedias, the atlases that cluttered up the corner cupboard near the blackboard, casting huge shadows. Then she opened two buttons of her blouse, and felt the secret little spot under her breast. Here, something was beating, furtive and regular.

Perhaps she hadn't been able to understand Brecht and the Berliner Ensemble... Perhaps her intelligence, by itself, was too narrow, limited, confused? Had she been presumptuous?

The image of a shrub in the shadow of a gigantic oak tree made her smile. Yes, she had spied not on 'the man she loved', but the man who 'had fascinated her'. Berlin glittered afar, in a world that was completely foreign to her. She had the impression she was coming back to herself, slowly, as if she were convalescing. Her inability to understand what was at stake, to understand the situation?... She had probably been too sensitive? Too sentimental? But all her energy, her 'pure and ardent heart' had led to those morose evenings. The night patrol, the ghostly, appeased world… Would she one day be able to justify herself for having spied on Brecht?

For such a long time, her inability to understand a world of polar opposites, cut and dried, dogmatic and cold, had reduced her to a ghost. She was an absence from the world. She knew that here, at least, with or without pupils, in the waning summer, in this slender blindspot of Time, she could get by and even smile. The violence of the world outside did not reach this schoolyard.

She went out, got into her Opel, the sky had cleared. There was still a misty haze hanging round the edge of the fir trees.

She drove towards the town centre. There was only the smooth road, the regular flowerbeds, white on each side. She drove unhurriedly down the avenues of a peaceful, familiar and inhabitable world. A road, a mere ribbon and regular white markings slipping by at the side.

She opened the gate to her house; the garden smelled nice.

mG 8/06

* NE5/06

ml

CB 11/06

12/05